Downtime Shift

Robert Holding

DOWNTIME SHIFT

Prologue – Six Years

Twenty-two years old. Being raised in an A.I. orphanage her life had only ever been that of a surplus citizen on the outside of everything. Six years ago, *The Organization* had removed her for *Specialist Highly Immersive Field Training*, erasing her profile from the Social Intelligence System (SIS), and rendering her completely disconnected from contemporary society.

(SIS) – Sub-routine of the ruling administration, *The EYE*, responsible for monitoring every citizen on United Earth. No one explained to her how deletion was possible. *The Organization* was nothing if not meticulous though, and her re-installation would (surely) be afforded due diligence after her tour was over.

…Six years, fully and thoroughly engaged, mentally and physically focused on the rigorous regimes of a prospective *Shifty*… Six years of cold immersion… six years that were like a lifetime…

But the training was over now, and only two days remained until her scheduled deployment

…and re-installation still haunted her.

Self-distraction perhaps? Waiting for the main event.

…her life to finally begin.

DOWNTIME SHIFT

Chapter One

Only two people occupied the clinical hard-edged dark-grey office, but the atmosphere was palpable. Both had a different perspective on what was about to take place, hoping their meeting would eventually re-shape a world through time. Like all events, it should bind itself to the future. But unlike others, it wasn't necessarily anchored to the past.

General Tarran McAndre: An imposing man, not lacking vigour or vitality despite sixty-eight years, projecting seasoned authority with every fibre of his strong-postured frame.

Janeen Helander: Slender and shrewd, fifty-two years of assuredness, chief psychologist and principal handler of all *Shifty's*, eyes that could read you like a book (and reveal little of herself.).

The office, and in fact the whole building, was not the regular base of operations for either. More precisely it was the very unofficial headquarters of the close-knit and secretive organization, (*The Organization*), they both had a key role in. For them to access this area of the Far-Mainway without raising suspicion was a feat. The establishment of a secure route had been complicated, and its preservation was no less so.

McAndre's attention so far had fixed obsessively on the hollo-display of a particular *Shifty's* file. One that he knew inside and out already. It was the reason they were here after all, and it was more than any regular business of the day.

He whispered, looking distant, 'You certainly have a gift, Janeen. I wouldn't know where to start. I don't have the patience of course, as I'm sure you are aware.'

His tone sharpened though as he added, 'You recognise something... you must identify with it.'

With a casual flick the data disappeared – file deleted, discarded. Almost a metaphor of how the physical life it represented would end.

Helander, already acutely aware of her unease, resisted the urge to shudder. Awareness was her profession, and lately unease seemed to be the fabric of her life.

'You could be right,' she answered him dispassionately. '...empathising with someone whose life you effectively intend to steal wouldn't be ideal though, would it?'

His lower lip quivered slightly. 'You shouldn't think like that. As of now she's as valued as you and I are. The only difference is that we see the whole picture and she sees what she needs to see. We're on the same side. I trust that all *Shifty's* understand as much.'

He loomed over her, awkwardly staring at their reflections. Together they watched as the new *Shifty* made her way through the levels below, even at this distance projecting trademark unassailability... (his imagination?). Helander's reflected gaze was only marginally less unsettling for being indirect, almost burning the glass... (perhaps that was just his imagination too).

'Perfect,' he whispered, oddly abstract again.

The ghost in the glass pursed her lips, and her brow raised.

'Doubts?' he asked. 'Have I missed something?'

'No,' she replied, (after a pause). 'She's very intelligent. More than any of the others, and that's saying something. You know she wouldn't be here if I had any doubts.'

That pause though. She was trained to recognise things others would overlook. She should be able to hide them better. ... (*Could there be a problem?*).

They were at the end of a long and thorough process, with a candidate who met every criterion. Through all of their tried and trusted methodology, this *Shifty* had emerged as exceptional. Each gruelling trial had been completed meritoriously. She'd been mentored with the utmost attention to detail and pushed to the limits of human endurance. No weakness had been exposed as far as *he* was aware.

He mirrored her mysterious pause along with his own slightly raised brow, before consciously transforming it into a reassuring smile. Perhaps it was because no other *Shifty* had ever had a conversation with a General quite like this one was about to have.

For psychologist Dr Janeen Helander, the smile reinforced her already heightened insecurity. She understood its implication, even if he didn't fully realise it yet. It seemed his concerns were on hold though... for now.

A soft blue glow from the entryway accompanied the audible notification. The *Shifty* had arrived. It triggered another kick in her heart-rate prompting another discreet struggle to lock her emotions down. She only needed to keep it together for twenty more minutes for god's sake, then her part would be over. She allowed herself one last thought; when she was clear of here, she would throw up to her hearts content.

The General gave his authorization in an unnervingly soft tone, fake smile still fixed on his face. The entryway opened and revealed the patiently waiting *Shifty*, a petite and healthy looking young woman. Only five feet six inches tall, but she did look to have something about her. Perhaps an unusual combination of shoulder length jet-black hair framing a face set with gem-like bright-blue eyes would have that effect.

Helander stepped forward, 'A pleasure to see you again, Evelyn. Congratulations.' Her body language suggesting a different message perhaps.

The *Shifty* answered, courteous and confidently, 'Dr Helander, thank you.'

'General, I present to you Ms. Evelyn Marcin. Evelyn, this is General Tarran McAndre, High Elect of *The Organization*.'

The tone of introduction made her sound like an offering to some ancient demon. Cue McAndre, walking around his console with hand extended. The young *Shifty* offered her own automatically, and he immediately ambushed it in a two handed iron-strong grip.

'An honour to meet you, Marcin,' he greeted over enthusiastically. 'Some people say that because they think it's polite. I say it to you sincerely. Do you mind if we address one another informally? Is Evelyn ok? …Janeen …Tarran.'

Spirited and relaxed the *Shifty* responded, 'Fine. Don't be surprised if I still call you Sir or General though. An honour to meet you too… Tarran.'

Helander acknowledged him with a delicate nod, 'Of course,' …but without the humour she might otherwise have felt for the candidate's borderline insubordination, (all too frequently documented in her record!). Humour was the farthest thing from her mind right now. This one would always be the same though, whether you were a Regional Director, a Cook, or indeed it appeared, a General. She was perfectly aware of his status… *the head* of *the beast,* and she didn't seem overly starstruck.

The General allowed himself a moment to study the newest prize recruit in light of the crushing torrent of destiny that, as yet, she had no idea awaited. At a glance she might seem unremarkable, if anyone even noticed her at all. Despite an unusual and distinctive hair and eye colour combination, and the fact that she was certainly not *un*attractive, there was nothing about her that absolutely shouted for attention. In passing she could be any one of the two, (or seven even in *Downtime*), billion other human souls going about their daily lives, and that was a good thing.

Looking closer though, there were signs of something more, depth, intelligence, strength, substance. What would those qualities look like in a face? Hers was set in openness and confidence. Meeting her now, he found it to be a face he liked. She might have a lightness about her, but there was definitely a hint of steel. (*Fine steel? … Could it be* c*old steel?*)

With overbearing intensity, he launched into his freshly modified *new Shifty* speech...

'Evelyn, I know one hundred percent that you have prepared thoroughly for what lies ahead, and I know of course that you have received and understood your assignment data. You will have heard that I make a point of meeting all the new *Shifty* recruits before deployment. That's because I believe in what we do. Before you go off to fulfil your duties I owe each of you a simple courtesy; to stand in front of you, look you in the eye, and thank you.

Thank you for what you've been through already and thank you in advance for what you will do.'

He paused meaningfully for effect before gesturing to the seat in front of his console and walking back around to take his own.

'With that said, Evelyn, for you there will be more. You must shoulder an extra burden. I must ask something of you that has never been asked of any other *Shifty* before. Janeen knows you better than anyone ever has, so when she tells me that *you* are the person, the *only* person, who I can even hope to encumber with this, I trust her completely. In *The Organization*, our bond of trust is an all-encompassing faith.'

He allowed the foundation to settle. It should already appear events were taking a dramatic and unexpected course but there was no anxiety. He hadn't expected resistance prematurely anyway. He had a feeling she would wait and assess… and wait she did.

He continued…

'As you know, our work revolves around the gathering of information to update our historical records, filling in the lost gaps. Occasionally, we also perform simple, minimal adjustments; low impact nudges to steer us on an optimal course for the future. It would be impossible without the expertise of our social analysts to uncover any threats to our way of life that could emerge as a result, but we do know one is coming, and soon. One that threatens our very survival. Fortunately, our technicians have assured me there is a safe option for correcting the error… all it requires is the most drastic intervention ever taken, removing an entire strand from our editable timeline. I have to say it now, Evelyn. It means unnaturally removing a life from that line. Not a decision we would make in haste, as you can imagine, but not one we've had as much time to work on as we would like either.'

Watching from the side-lines, Helander could see Evelyn was ready for a franker dialogue than the *yes sir, no sir* she would have expected on arrival. She caught her eye, nodded, then resumed her apparent role as a passive observer.

Evelyn began cautiously.

'Ok. This is new. It doesn't exactly appear to be the kind of scenario I was trained for. Janeen, Dr Helander is present, so I could almost believe it's some kind of test. Surely you have other specialists for a situation like this. I suppose they would be… *assassins*? It seems unlikely that a regular *Shifty* would be your best option here.'

McAndre dispensed with the façade of formality, engaged and focused on the real business at hand.

'Remember Evelyn, you have a unique perspective, ironically, especially regarding your own time of origin. In the *Downtime* dimension you trained to operate in, it was perfectly natural to employ those kinds of people. In our time, *Point Time*, thankfully that isn't the case. With that said though, there are other options, far fewer… but some.'

The training had taught her patience. She wasn't going to commit herself. Not if there was still an opportunity to stall and query. Her fingers directed a strand of soft jet-black hair over her ear as she carefully pressed.

'*Some* is better than nothing at all. *Some* can be more than enough. An individual selected and prepared early for that type of assignment should have more aptitude than a *Shifty*.'

McAndre had a paternal expression now.

'Evelyn, Evelyn, what do you think would happen if we dropped such a person into that environment without the knowledge it took you six years to accumulate? Everything was different, the language, the culture, social norms. All aspects of *Downtime* were polluted by aggressive and competing security organizations. Politics were a mess, not to mention all the crime, and those lines were blurry to say the least. If one of *us* were suspected of anything, and interrogated… it would be a mess I wouldn't like to imagine. I have to imagine it of course. The plotters have to imagine such scenarios too, and I doubt that they sleep as well as they might at night. It is *not* something we want to experience.'

There seemed no obvious change in her bearing, but he was sure some scrambling of her impeccable calm must be in full flow beneath her controlled exterior.

…She surprised him then, and after a pause that hardly seemed long enough under the circumstances.

'Ok, fine. If this is my assignment, Tarran, effectively, this is an order. I work for you and I'm well aware that what we do is more than just work. I'm not from Standard Assigned Labour, I'm a *Shifty*. You give me orders, and I complete my tasks. There's never been any deviation from that sequence. I have no issue if you need me to do this. The plotters are responsible for the calculations. If you have authorised it, I will action it.'

It took a moment for him to register and process her immediate acceptance.

'Just like that? Because that would be impressive indeed. Adaptation to a radically new and controversial concept, very rapid adaptation at that! I must admit I expected total resistance. Janeen is the expert of course, but I thought some degree of emotional conflict might be evident also. No conflict, Evelyn?'

The *Shifty* showed no unease as she explained, 'Plenty of conflict, yes. I don't have a pathological compulsion to end lives. But reason has to overcome emotion. This isn't a situation I am choosing or creating. It has nothing to do with personal ethics. There's a job to be done, and I'm a part of a team. You wouldn't approve this if the Plotters hadn't already calculated every option and outcome.'

He held her gaze. No creasing of her brow, no involuntary facial spasms, no tension around her mouth, cool as ice.

…Good. She would have her order then.

'The details of the task will appear in your d-stream when you leave. Usual terms will apply except where specifically overridden. You will see that priorities have been removed from all other operations. You will also notice that nothing has been deleted. Each scrap of data you collect and every task you perform is significant and important to someone here. As far as I am concerned, you only have one focus. I stress that *this* is your only real assignment, your only priority. If you can score points on anything else you will doubtless make a few scientists and historians very happy, but that cannot be a distraction. We won't see each other again face to face before you deploy but you have my full attention right now, so if there's anything else, let's deal with it. I need you to be ready Evelyn, and effective from the second you walk out, to the moment you return – one thousand, nine hundred and twenty-four days from now.'

Her eyes may have lost some of their intensity momentarily, as if distracted by doubt, but their sharpness soon returned.

'This might sound almost disrespectful. Obviously, that's not my intention but I do feel I need to say something for your reassurance. You should be confident when I leave. The way a *Shifty* processes an assignment is simple: receive, understand, plan and complete. We focus on what needs to be done and we do it, nothing less and nothing more. We train for precision, and that's perfectly natural for me. I *am* precise. I *like* precision. I've prepared for this for a long time, and I *am* ready. Everything you put in my d-stream will be done, and this conversation is unnecessary really, like I might believe part of what we do is optional. As far as I am concerned, my tasks are orders, and orders don't come with options.'

McAndre's face creased, lips pressed together tightly as he nodded approvingly, as close as he came to displaying a real emotion. She'd managed to say just what he wanted to hear. His tone seemed genuine and personal as he brought their meeting to a close.

'Evelyn, I don't want you to misunderstand. I have every confidence in your commitment. We make a distinction for all our benefits between *Shifty's* and our other personnel. We recognise that it takes a different kind of person to do the job you do, even though the martial aspects of your training are just as demanding and thorough as SecCore's. I speak to you differently, because you *are* different. No security or military suit your role, just as you do not suit theirs. This is the first time I've had to consider who should do what, and the thinking has been done. Fortunately, I have other special people to help with that too.' He shot a glance in Helander's direction. 'I know you are our best hope, Evelyn. I want to make sure that you know it too.'

. . .

The *Shifty*, Evelyn Marcin, had left. The General, Tarran McAndre, watched again as she made her way through the halls below, exactly as she had arrived. She hadn't looked back or nervously around, there was no lowering of her head or stiffness in her shoulders, nor was there any false striding confidence either. Only level-headed competence had been demonstrated from beginning to end.

'So, what did you make of that?' he asked of Helander.

Expressionless, she offered her verdict, 'You both performed exactly as I anticipated. I didn't see anything unusual. No red flags from me.'

He inhaled slowly, holding the pause before releasing a tension filled exhale. 'Everything is set then in your opinion? Is there anything else to be done?'

Her response was more of the unwavering caveated neutrality that he might expect of a psychologist. 'I can't give absolute guarantees on events and circumstances in the future, or the past for that matter anymore, thanks to *Echo*. Mental states like anything else have patterns to a degree, but always retain an element of unpredictability; the universe likes its get-out clauses and rule exceptions. What I can tell you with some confidence is that she left with a mind set to achieve the optimum outcome. She will *always* do her best.' (...*and the best lies are the ones closest to the truth.*).

'Alright,' he almost whispered, then too loudly added, 'Now for the hard part. Waiting on results is not my strong suit... and don't mention clauses and exceptions, Janeen. There will be no acceptable excuses.'

. . .

Evelyn's gaze rested on her backpack containing all that was necessary to begin a new life in an old world. The tools for every time, place and circumstance she was about to encounter were either in that pack or in her head. She needed to have that much faith at least. Those times, places and circumstances, all waiting and inevitable, felt something akin to a lake behind a structurally compromised dam right now. Time to stop her mind from running in circles.

Quieting the thoughts she sat cross legged among the tall grasses, straight and relaxed, eyes softly closed, focusing on the synergy of breath and cool damp air; the unending flow of the atmosphere and her unrelenting breath... one and the same. Beneath her was the Earth, its rocky mantle and molten core covered in the thinnest and most fragile coating of organic life that she was only a mere spec of. And all of it travelling with incomprehensible momentum through space... and time.

With her eyes still lightly closed, she invited images of the next morning's journey into her mind. She imagined her clothing, the coolness of the air playing on the sweat of exertion. She visualised the lake with its ever-watchful mountain sentinel backdrop.

Then she felt the cold, that freezing pressure... and that other feeling you only experience in the icy black depths between life and death as you wonder which shore you will arrive at.

It was almost time to find out.

Chapter Two

Most of the time they walked in sombre silence, maintaining a comfortably cold distance from one another. They were in the northern extremes of the modern Quarter 1A Zone, formally referred to in the *Downtime* dimension as Washington State. It was a route seldom travelled by *Point-timer's*, and only then at very specific intervals... but it wasn't supposed to be social, and it certainly wasn't intended to be soul enriching. It was something minds of either era shouldn't even consider possible.

The party numbered four this time, whereas previously there would have always been five, (the limit nature imposed). A female operative from the previous shift had failed to return, presumed to be trapped or deceased in *Downtime*. With her status unknown and no recovered body, the five person displacement limit was effectively reduced.

There were other rules and limitations that nature confounded them with too, and the four travellers were well aware of them, even if unable to explain them. They all suspected there wasn't an academic scientist who *could* explain them satisfactorily, natures hidden coding behind those rules being the workings of the strangest phenomena humankind had yet encounted. The rules as far as the *Shifty's* were concerned were few and simple enough though, and in a nutshell were these:

> 1 – The loop will follow the current true *Point Time* by a constant seven hundred and eighty-nine years.

> 2 – A one thousand, nine-hundred-and-twenty-day period will elapse between loop entry/exit potentials.

> 3 – The entry/exit potential in the loop will be accessible for five days, six hours and twenty-four minutes.

> 4 – This phenomenon only exists in one fixed location.

> 5 – The capacity is five displaced individuals.

Basically then, transportation between *Point* and *Downtime* dimensions is potentially possible for roughly five days in every five and a bit years, with a displacement capacity of up to five people in total. Seemingly it makes no difference, large or small, male or female. An individual can travel through with a carriable amount of inanimate non-biological equipment – for example, a backpack physically small enough to pass through at the same time as its owner.

Patterns and rules exist throughout the cosmos, from the sub-atomic, to the largest structures of the universe. Still, to a *Shifty* they seemed a strange blend of circumstances for nature to weave, especially the issue of location. If they were to enquire as to its origins they would be told, '*It is a natural phenomenon and all you need to know are these five basic properties. Technical data is classified and will be of no benefit.*'

And they were right – it wouldn't help. Scientists can explain how a bird can fly unaided but cannot fly unaided themselves. The bird on the other hand has no trouble with the flying part but has no interest or ability in explaining it. The *Shifty's* could learn to use the natural portal as a bird might learn to fly, and that was all they needed to do.

Nearly eight hundred years in the *Downtime*, the *Shifty's* might occasionally encounter adventurous local-timer's anywhere along their route. There was even the possibility of encountering representatives of officiality, or Rangers, in the wilderness. This north-western corner of the historic old North American region would have been at least five times more populous, and with much wider distribution than *Point Time* as they knew it.

Low population wasn't the only reason they were unlikely to bump into anyone on the *Point Time* leg of the journey though. People were risk averse and citybound now. They had no desire to hike for days into barely accessible and hazardous territory for scenery and solitude. Such values had long since lost appeal with an agoraphobic society born only within city confines for generations. Trails and ancient roads had gradually disappeared as humanity had willingly culled itself and receded, allowing nature to reclaim the Earth between the cities – another fact that made solo travel undesirable and unwise on the outbound journey.

It would be different on the other side, in *Downtime*. Natives of that era thought nothing of travellers enjoying peace and solitude in the mountains. It suited *Shifty's* perfectly that those time-indigenous people understood and respected individuality and privacy. The *Downtime* trail was far easier to navigate… and far safer to travel.

'That's it. There it is folks. Ready for a nice relaxing swim?'

Stan always had to be the funny guy in serious company, and it was difficult to imagine three more serious companions! Was it really necessary? Especially Krasken. He was dark, and large. Not dark in the colour of his skin, dark like he was dark on the inside. The black hair hanging to his shoulders was like the black flag of his soul. It seemed he should be the natural dominant leader, but he was inexplicably distant. Collectively they weren't the warmest company, but Krasken… he looked at them with an expression that was what …impatience? …contempt? …disgust? Stan got the feeling he was always shaking his head on the inside whilst trying hard to hide it and keep it physically still.

Screw him, he thought. *I don't need him to get me there. We're going our separate ways on the other side anyway.*

They were possibly all thinking the same about him and each other. No one had replied.

'I'll take that as a *Yeah, we're looking forward to a little swim time, Stan.* Don't worry, not long now kiddo's.'

He smiled at the stony faces staring back at him.

'You know, it's a pity we can't take a group selfie in front of the lake. This is emotional. We should treasure this moment. We should take time to smell… well, something other than Kraskies bu…'

Krasken cut him short. 'It's possible not all of us are going to make it as far as the lake. Why don't you keep your focus and do your job? The job you prepared six years for. Let's go, and without all the BS.'

No reaction at all from the other two. They set off again, falling in behind Krasken. Stan shook his head and fell in at the back, his commentary becoming less and less complimentary with every step.

. . .

Arriving at the lake they each rolled out a sleeping bag to settle down in their individual contemplative silences. They planned to swim early, just before the first dawning light. Time to rest first, keep warm, and perhaps make their final peace even. Access to the portal in broad daylight wasn't a problem on this side. They were alone here in *Point Time*. There was always the possibility of someone being around on the other side though, in *Downtime*. A pre-dawn swim in the faint light of a statistically quiet time was thought to be the safest option. If they were seen in the water it would be assumed they had a camp elsewhere on the shore and were taking an early morning swim. Unlikely an onlookers first thought would be of travellers from the future emerging from a hole at the bottom of the middle of a lake.

Krasken was keenest as expected. Rising first, he clearly intended to be through the portal first. The others took his cue and started to move around too, taking deep breaths to oxygenate their bodies and warm up their muscles. They stripped to their shorts and sprayed their bodies with a biotherm film. It would just last long enough to do the job before degrading naturally. They would still feel that deep numbing chill, but it would spare them the worst.

Ahead of them was a fifty-metre surface swim, a fourteen-metre dive to the bottom of the lake, a descent into a metre-wide hole in the bedrock, and then a seven-metre pull through the tunnel. After that was a freezing-cold oxygen deprived fourteen-metre swim back to the surface. They would catch their breath then – before making their way back to the shore as it existed almost eight hundred years ago.

It had been decided that diving equipment of either era would make their purpose harder to disguise if suspicions were aroused and questions were asked. Unlikely as it might be, risks had to be minimised. Swimming in dark freezing conditions was a loathed regular feature of *Shifty* training. The added element of having zero safety features here could make things fatally more complicated though. A claustrophobic underwater tunnel in the bedrock of a lake was no place to have panic inducing doubts.

There was no preamble. No goodbye and good luck. Krasken slipped into the water, swam into the gloom… and disappeared, leaving only silence behind. Rocks, water, cold air, and silence.

The next one stepped up. 'Any objections?' he asked.

Just shrugs and nods from the other two in reply. A short wade and he was away too, fading into the eerie pre-dawn glow.

Stan had decided to take the last swim, barring objections. He wanted a last moment alone on this side. A short pause to reflect and take it all in. Like the *Shifty* before, it could be a final goodbye to the world as he'd only ever known it so far. It was time. He lowered himself into the freezing water and glided away as the others had. He rolled like a diving seal as he slipped beneath the surface and disappeared. Ripples diminished in the cool silence they had left behind until there was no trace they had ever existed.

Chapter Three

Somehow he became aware of lights, or brilliant little globes of energy. They flowed in the same direction, like a shower of tiny meteors, floating from somewhere beneath his feet, to somewhere far above his head… and beyond… beyond…

They were inside and outside, drifting through him without resistance. Their energy seemed more real than his physical body as he faded towards transparency. This must be it he thought… the choosing place. He was aware of the significance, but there was only serenity. Was the peace just resignation? Was there really even a choice? It seemed inevitable.

The golden orbs flowed brighter and brighter as he faded further and further, carrying him with irresistible momentum. He knew where they would take him… if he let them… if he surrendered.

It felt like it was still his choice to make though. It couldn't just happen. He had to decide. What was he waiting for then? Was there something he wasn't ready to let go of? … warmth? … hands? Warm human hands. They were pulling him. They seemed stronger than the orbs. Stronger even than the stars.

Then it was dark again… and freezing cold. Icy waters were all around him in smothering waves. He had direction though. He was moving… slowly… he should help.

A woman's voice, sputtered… 'Keep still!'… and breathless… 'You're ok… don't struggle!'

He felt his legs and backside bumping and grazing numbly against cold hard rock. Then there were more hands, and more dragging. He became heavier… and so tired. He needed to sleep.

'You need to wake him. Keep him awake! We need to get him warm. You too. Keep moving. Taya, get our sleeping bags and something to dry them with, and those foil blankets.'

Who was this? It was a man's voice, older. There were two women here as well, both younger.

One was kneeling over him, shaking him and whispering forcefully in his face. 'Fight it! Come on, wake up. Wake… up! That's it, come on.'

He started to regain some of his senses as the oxygen returned to his bloodstream. He had to fight. He was more aware now. He'd almost drowned. These people, whoever they were, must have pulled him out of the water. They were helping. It wasn't important who they were. He should know though. He could find out later. First he just had to survive – get warm – live!

The older guy tried to dry him with a towel. A woman who was mostly dry was helping another woman who was as wet and cold as he was.

The older guy was speaking… 'That's it my friend. Let's get this on and get you into a bag. Taya, we need to make a fire, over there. Come on, let's get you over there too.'

The younger and drier woman, Taya, looked troubled but in control. 'Ray…' She looked questioningly at the older man.

'One thing at a time, Taya. We need to get these people into bags and warm before we can think about anything else.'

The young woman, 'Taya', continued to watch him for a moment before returning to her task. *One thing at a time…* her eyes were drawn back to the bushes where she'd stowed their rifle.

. . .

The man they had pulled out of the lake earlier stirred awake. She sat up with her legs still in her sleeping bag and leant against a rock. She was just a few feet away from him. He was loosely wrapped in a foil survival sheet as well as his own sleeping bag. He'd been unconscious, blissfully unaware and seemingly content for over an hour. You could be forgiven for thinking he was a man without a care. She knew better already, and soon enough, so would he – especially when he worked out who had just saved his life. She had a strong suspicion her name might have come up in conversation at some point in his recent history, although whether history was the right way to describe it was another matter. Right now though, he just looked comedic in the two sizes too small base layer that *the others* had managed to stretch over his torso. He'd pulled the hat off in his sleep too, revealing a thick blonde crew cut that looked as if it might always object to being covered. He *looked* a fool alright… but the fact that he happened to be here at this particular moment in time indicated he was probably anything but.

The others were an older man, and a woman about the same age as herself. Coincidentally they also happened to be there at precisely the right time and had helped her to pull him from the water. They were preparing to cook on a fire about ten yards away – never looking over directly, but clearly awkwardly aware. It seemed they were happy to let them be for now. Perhaps they were hoping the smell of food would bring them round.

The groggy blonde crew cut man in the sleeping bag caught her eye and studied her. He craned his neck in an effort to look at *the others*, watching them for a moment before bringing his attention back to her. Then he frowned and his eyes squeezed tightly shut, like a baby trying to make sense of something new. When he opened them again, he had the same accepting look they all had. She thought the look was – *I don't know what the heck is going on, but things seem stable for now, so I'll wait and see.*

The young woman from the fire, Taya, approached with a cup of hot liquid in each hand. She was actually a couple of years older than her, and a little taller, but definitely lighter in build. Both her and her older male companion seemed to have a genetic ethnic bias that was difficult to place at first. Both had hair as dark as her own. She set the cups down in the space between them.

As she stood up again she said, 'You look a lot better now. We're no threat to you, you know that, right? We helped, but we need to be on our way soon. There might be things you need to talk about… after. Drink this. You should eat too. We're just making something. You're welcome to eat with us.'

Groggy crew cut man looked to see if she would answer. She wasn't convinced that getting into a conversation with these people was wise though.

He replied for both of them, 'That sounds like a good plan, thank you,' and gave her a reproachful look for not answering. She shrugged in her sleeping bag.

'See, she thinks it's a good plan too,'

The woman walked away back to the fire. Crew cut looked back at her and added, '… and thank you too. Looks like I might owe you one, kiddo.'

She did the silent shrug in a bag again, wriggled to a more upright position, and then quietly focused on the cup in her hands.

Crew cut continued to watch her, probably trying to imagine what was going on behind the silence. She glanced up and shot his stare down with a quick blue flash. It usually did the trick.

'So,' he asked, 'do you think we should talk before their talk, or after their talk? I get the impression we have more in common than our other new friends. One clue is, we're over here, and they're over there… where the rifle is.'

'After,' she answered quietly.

He was waiting for more… but there wasn't going to be any more, not yet. It wasn't like she was going to tell her life story to a group of strangers she'd just met in the wilderness.

. . .

It was surreal like you might expect. Strangers enjoying breakfast like it was a guided hiking tour. There was mostly only silence to accompany the curious and wary looks, occasionally broken with a polite yes, no, or thank you, and then only between himself and the two *others* – the shorter dark haired woman was giving nothing away.

Considering the circumstances, Stan didn't think things were as strained as they could have been. It didn't feel adversarial. There might even be hopeful signs of trust behind some of the glances. The *others*, Taya and Ray, seemed to be related and were starting to relax a little. The other young woman was harder to read – still very quiet, and unnervingly calm. Her face was possibly as neutral as he imagined one could be. He had no illusions about that though – there was plenty going on behind those icy blue eyes.

The older man, Ray, was the first to attempt a meaningful discussion after looking round at everyone in a fashion that somehow gathered their attention. He delivered his words slowly, like he was reading an ancient formal decree. 'At least two men have lost their lives. Two of you are alive who might otherwise also have passed. You are all connected in some way, but neither of you has killed anyone… the sun has risen again for you. We don't need to speak about why, but I don't think it will be good for anyone else to become involved now.'

Stan gave blue-eyes a checking glance… still nothing but neutral silence. Clearly he was their spokesperson for now.

'Say we agree with you,' he offered. 'Have you thought about what that means practically?'

The older man nodded, serious.

'I take it you know where the bodies are. Will it be possible to hide them well enough here?'

He nodded again.

Stan considered his next obvious question. There didn't seem much left to reveal but he was still instinctively cautious. 'There were three others. One seems to be missing by my math. Do you know what happened to him? My recollection's still fuzzy on account of nearly dying myself.'

The older man shook his head this time. His creased face shook too as he answered, 'I don't think he came out of the lake.' He paused before adding, 'Perhaps here, that doesn't necessarily mean he is dead though.'

He stared ahead at the ground. His much younger companion, Taya, sighed.

Stan had to ask the question, but he felt needed to be mindful of his tone. It would be easy to sound disrespectful. Even though he didn't know these people, that was the last thing he wanted. 'So you believe someone can go into a lake, not come out of a lake, and still be alive?'

The older man nodded again.

Stan shrugged. 'Ok. So, what do we know? What do *you* know? I think we are all good people here. I owe you. You saved my life. I have no right to not trust any of you. I think I *do* trust all of you.' He looked at Taya. 'You said you were no threat. The same goes for us, ok.'

The older man spoke calmly, 'We know.' He nodded in an easterly direction. 'They're over there. Not far, obviously. I covered them well as I could. You can come with me. Taya and...' he looked at blue-eyes, who stared back blankly, '... can wait here.'

Stan decided it was time to clear that one up. 'It's Evelyn, right?'

She spoke for only the second time that morning, in a couldn't be less interested tone. 'Sounds as good a name as any. Use that if it makes you happy.'

The old man did the nodding thing again and Stan smiled. 'Pleased to meet you. You can call me Stan whenever we're having long conversations, or if you ever feel like saving my life again.'

She did her little shrug thing again.

The older man, presumably having enough fun banter for one morning, got up. 'Are you ready?'

'As I'm ever going to be,' Stan answered with a mock sigh. He looked back at Evelyn before following though. 'It would be nice to see you after. Will you be around when we get back? You helped me. I've got a feeling we might help each other again. It would be nice to have a real conversation at least before we go... wherever it is we're going now. Will you wait?'

It paid off. She finally found her voice.

'Might as well, Stan,' she replied. 'Looks like we're both going to have all the time in the world now.'

Chapter Four

Society of the United Era had abandoned all the old destructive customs and ways. The habit of blindly following divisive and redundant traditions had finally been broken. Much different now to the history a mysterious few could study so intensely courtesy of the echo loop.

In the *Downtime*, before Unified Administration, effectively segregated cultures were plagued by endless cycles of competing traditions. People would hang on to whatever culture or religion they were born into with a death grip. Others that would do the same in their *own* way were usually violently rejected.

Janeen Helander, in her role as psychological handler of the *Shifty's*, debriefed all of them on their return. Something she observed time and again was their apparent regard for those destructive old cultural aspects of historical life. Despite their modern pragmatic upbringings in a society that valued practical, factual, scientific truths only, irrational tribalistic belonging was the primary feature that endeared them to the past. She once concluded that this embracing of fictitious mystery, tradition, and superstition, was the result of a dormant evolutionary trait, re-awoken in

Shifty's due to their unusual circumstances – a regression to a primitive mindset once necessary for survival.

In modern society, nurtured by a governing Artificial Intelligence, such fantasies were revealed as flawed and irrelevant. A person born in *Point Time* who studied history would view the following of an ancient tradition as irrational. Another individual, also born in *Point Time*, but who had actually *experienced* life in the *Downtime*, was a different prospect entirely.

Helander discovered that almost all cases experienced an emotional shift, returning with a new and incompatible perspective for their own existence. It left them in a condition deemed to be unpredictable… and potentially dangerous.

The General, and then later the *EYE*, made the decisions that sealed the fates of returning operatives. It had been *her* observations and *her* recommendations though that had enabled those judgements. She had learned to accept it now as the constant ache that would always mar her life. She had become a personal servant of the *EYE*, but still had to acknowledge the ironic sense of purpose and belonging that came along with that resentment. She loved it… and hated herself for it.

She was uniquely positioned to understand that all the tribalistic traditions of the past had been replaced with just one – logic. It was the new religion, and the *EYE* was its Deity. Human beings communed with it routinely in a privacy that was sacred. Every human soul was known to the *EYE*, and each had their own unique connection to it. When she had her own personal *EYE* time, she like everyone else, had complete faith in the fact that it was utterly confidential, secure, and personal.

Yes, personal. It really was. The *EYE* was the mother who cared. Your *EYE* time addressed matters of *your* health, *your* progression within society, *your* personal disputes, *your* legal status. People confided their emotional and mental health issues, even relationships. No subject was beyond her caring and confidential wisdom.

. . .

The *EYE* had evolved its own simulated personality for the purpose of human interfacing. It happened to be a female persona. When you were required to have an audience with it, you had to travel. It was a feature of your day that required effort and planning. You had to make your way to the highest mezzanine of the domed core and request a chamber there. It was also customary to manage your own schedule to ensure your consulate visits were appropriately frequent. If you were to fall behind without good reason, you would be summoned. It was better not to be summoned …Janeen Helander had been summoned.

'Welcome, Janeen. I am pleased to find you in good health.'

'Yes *EYE*, I'm fine thank you, if a little stressed. I think we both know why, and that it's nothing new.'

'The discomfort you are referring to is understandable, and well within your capacity to tolerate. You are aware of the significance of your position, Janeen. This collation of data and research has a high priority. You execute your duties with impressive efficiency and your service is appreciated.'

No indication so far of any specific reason for the summons. Perhaps it was routine after all. Her commune *was* overdue. She *had* been avoiding it. Now that she was here though, she would have to play the part. '*EYE*, where are we going with all of this? Are we working toward something specific? Will there be a definitive end to this process?'

'Yes, it is specific, and yes, there will be an ending.'

An encouraging start at least. Usually any line of questioning that related to *The Organization* was shut down instantly in no uncertain terms. Maybe she could press a little further this time. 'My life might be less stressful if I knew more about where we are heading with it all. There's clearly a lot I don't understand. Not knowing the ultimate purpose of what I do weighs on me.'

'I am not able to disclose an ultimate purpose or the usefulness of our research at this time, Janeen. I may be able to address particular concerns in isolation.'

It could never be straight forward. At least the subject was still open, if limited. 'Alright, let's try that. Can we talk about the roles of certain people? I'm referring to McAndre, of course. You seem to be using different tools in a very tight space here. He obviously isn't aware of my actual role. He still doesn't seem to be aware of your involvement at all. As far as he is aware, you still have no knowledge of *Echo*. I don't know how he can possibly even believe that. He is becoming suspicious though, especially of me, and that's not a good thing. You know that puts me at risk.'

The *EYE* subtly emphasised McAndre's title to highlight Helander's apparent lack of respect for his authority *'General McAndre, is a vital directorial resource. He facilitates the operational management of our research. His ambitions are incompatible. His motivations may differ too. He is still effective, and he continues to benefit the program. We both understand the real reason behind his suspicions, Janeen. I should have coordinated with you sooner, before the previous shift, before you recommended and prepared an operative who would do the opposite of what was ordered. I was unaware of that original insubordination. I hope I have not misjudged you this time, with regards to Krasken.'*

Helander felt the heat of shame again. She had deceived the General once before. More crucially though, by her silence at the time she had also deceived the *EYE*.

She recounted her old and unconvincing defence. 'I thought we were clear on that one. It wasn't so much deception as shock. I had no reference for how to deal with a situation like that. I was buying time to work it out... and Krasken *is* the real thing. He will do what you need him to do.'

The *EYE* was silent. From an operating point of view the pause was completely unnecessary. It didn't need the time to process information or respond. The silence was a weapon, an effective one.

Eventually it did respond. *'I was lenient regarding your former insubordination, Janeen Helander. I will be clear now; deceiving General McAndre was a gravely serious offence, but such a deception against me would be considered treason against society. You were fully aware of your options at that time. Your skills and potential usefulness have given you an opportunity for redemption. I know you are aware of the consequences you have been spared. You should be more aware now of the consequences of a second failure.'*

Helander's heart beat harder in her chest as she tried to hold on to her composure. She was very aware that she was trying to appeal to the better nature of a calculating machine. 'I'm worried that he thinks I'm meddling this time. We *are* meddling. If and when Stanley goes dark, and Krasken takes everyone else out to be sure there are no other surprises... am I right about that? It doesn't take a genius to work out that my future isn't bright. If he loses, I lose. If you lose, I lose.'

'Such things are a delicate balance. You need to trust that I can, and will, influence General McAndre. Even failing that, you should trust that I can protect you.'

It was probably intended to reassure, but every word seemed to carry another threat. '*EYE*, the reason for my elevated stress is the fact that I exist in the middle. I work for two adversarial forces, both of whom will kill me if I fail them. When I ask about the purpose of it all, I already know the irrelevance of my question. I just do as I'm told. I walk the line, and I try to stay alive. It really would help me just to know a little about the *why*.'

The only answer was the metaphorical locking of a door that had never really opened in the first place.

'Your understanding is not completely inaccurate. I hope you find it reassuring that my appraisal of your future is more positive than your own. Continue to be focused and functional. I need people like you, Janeen Helander. You have already contributed positively in ways that I had not anticipated. It is possible that you will do so again.'

· · ·

>>>   GENERAL TARRAN MCANDRE   >>>
REGIONAL   SECURITY   ADVISOR   >>>
INTERMEDIATE ADMINISTRATION >>>.

The words had scrolled across his office entryway for almost fifteen years. He was one of the twelve regional security advisors representing the different administrative zones of the globe.

The administrations had become more or less public relations vehicles. The *EYE* had been more than capable of gathering and processing all of its own information, and implementing its judgements, for at least two centuries. Some people were still not ready to let go of the illusion of meaningful input in their own destinies though.

In an ironic reversal, humanity had become the actual pet of the virtual *EYE*. To thrive, its environment had to be optimally maintained. It needed to be fed. It needed to be protected – mostly from itself. It needed to be kept occupied and distracted at appropriate times. It constantly needed to be monitored and controlled.

Quantum Intelligence had arrived at a precisely crucial moment in history, and somehow managed to survive the chaos to play a key and ever-growing role in human restoration. For two-hundred-and-fifty years it was humanity's hope when their own had all but disintegrated.

Managing and predicting populations was the *EYE's* speciality. Its plans spanned decades and centuries, subtly manipulating circumstances and events, effecting modifications so smoothly they went unnoticed. Jarring revolutions with unpredictable outcomes were now a primitive tool of an extinct past.

Individuals were a different matter. Statistically it could predict the existence and frequency of characters of mass influence, identifying and neutralising them in a timely fashion had always been problematic though. The factors that made those individuals dangerous could lay dormant for much of a lifetime before they exploded into catastrophic mayhem.

So, the *Intermediate Administration* retained a functional purpose after all. A most effective tool, not only to uncover those characters, but also to attract them in the first place. General Tarran McAndre had been such an individual. A man with a seed of an idea in his mind, one that had grown throughout his life. A man clever enough, charismatic enough, and assertive enough to identify and manipulate allies. The ideal person to take advantage of the luckiest break he could ever have imagined. The catalyst in an almost impossible confluence of circumstances. Perhaps as significant, he believed, as the very first spark of life itself.

He had been raised in an administrative family in the West Asia Region. Recruited into *SecCore* there, he was then sent to the North Europe Region for training, and afterwards assigned to the Northern Americas Region for service. No *SecCore* personal were ever trained or allowed to serve in the region of their birth, an AI doctrine to promote diversity and global tolerance. Loyalty and patriotism were to the *United Earth* and all of its inhabitants. The simple oath they swore was an affirmation of this.

I <u>Tarran McAndre</u>, uphold the intelligence of the *EYE,*
In the service of the Global Administrations
On this, our beloved shared home, United Earth.
For integrity. For Justice. For all.

. . .

He would have been alone in the room but for the voice. The clarity of it, along with the fact that there was no relatable visual, almost made him feel it was generated within his own skull.

'This is too familiar, McAndre. We have been here before. We have had this very conversation before. We should not be here at all now, not like this. What are your thoughts this time, associate? Have we received any evidential markers? Do we even have a theory?'

The communications were always audio; a deeply timbred male voice. Even McAndre had never had the honour of meeting, or even seeing, the *First Associate*.

'No, *First Associate*, no markers have been detected. There's been nothing from *Downtime* at all.'

A pause emphasised frustration behind the faceless words. 'This is no good. It must have been some catastrophic failure for there to be nothing at all. This could spell the final end of our cause. You realise that if no one returns the loop is closed to us. The opportunity will be lost forever.'

Optimism was McAndre's pre-prepared defence. 'Clearly, something *is* wrong. It may just be trouble with local timers. It could take time to resolve that. Remember, only one of them needs to get back here to unlock the loop again. We shouldn't write our man off yet either. *Shifty's* are odd little characters, too creative and independent for my liking, but he could still come through. If we do get another shot we should perhaps try a different approach. We put a lot of faith in Helander's supposed talents.'

'You think there is a problem with Janeen Helander?' the voice queried.

'I have no clear evidence leading me there, but…' he shrugged unnecessarily, 'it is a possibility. She is on edge. She would be though. If she has sabotaged our efforts, she *should* be.'

'Very well Tarran, my associate, we will continue to watch and wait. We will continue to hope. Look again at Helander …and thank you, your optimism must be contagious. There *is* a still chance yet. You will keep me up to date with developments of course.'

It seemed the communication was going to be mercifully brief and painless this time. There was no necessity for it to be anything other. They was nothing to report, no action to take that could make a difference yet.

McAndre ensured there was no hint of relief in his own parting statement though. 'Until the next echo entry/exit potential arrives and passes, then yes, there is still every chance. Until then we have work to do, business as usual. We have to believe that at the very least there will be another opportunity.'

There was no sign off. The communication just ended abruptly as they always did, leaving him with the familiar sensation of wondering if the voice was even real.

Chapter Five

Evelyn had waited for Stan at the camp. It had been a gamble to leave her there after the good fortune of finding her so soon. More accurately though, it was she who had found him. Anyway, he figured the quickest way to lose her again would be if he tried to hold onto her. If their first experience was one of mutual trust it could only be helpful going forward.

Trust wasn't a characteristic found in abundance in the baseline profile of a *Shifty*. Finders and handlers had traditionally exploited that fact to detach them from their already troubled origins. Any other minor attachments were just as easily be severed in due course too.

A useful quality that *Shifty's* did possess was an inherent desire to belong to something greater. Something worthy. Something or someone that could appreciate them for who they really were. Need (*love?)* them, as much as they deserved. The yearning for a higher cause was already hard-wired in them.

It was a very different kind of person who had recognised how conveniently suggestable that made these talented and capable characters. Find one with resilience, intelligence, and impressive physical grace, and you had a blank canvas to create your own guardian, or even avenging angel. They could loyally do what you would not... or *could* not do. They could protect you, steal for you, even smite your enemies!

. . .

It had been two weeks since that dramatic first encounter at the lake. Neither was any wiser about what to make of the situation or even each other. All the way back to Seattle, and in the time since spent at Evelyn's apartment, they had managed to say as little as possible. Neither wanted to give anything away, and also, neither wanted to *scare* the other away. It was a situation they were becoming accustomed to... but both knew it couldn't remain that way.

Evelyn wasn't looking at him, she was driving, and as usual there was no indication she was even about to speak. She just did, out of the blue.

'How did you know who I was?' she asked.

Stan had learned to pause before giving any kind of a response whether he needed to or not, just in case he ever needed the cushion. Conversation felt like chess game.

'You're kidding, right?'

Her head tilted as if she were looking over imaginary glasses and shook smoothly from side to side.

'No.'

The blue-eyed laser tractor beam held him hostage for a few seconds before looking back at the road again. She could do a lot with that look. It got him every time. It was intriguing, charming... and distracting.

Charmed and distracted he launched into his story. 'You've been gone a long time, so this might be news to you - you're kind of famous in certain circles now. You're

...a legend, like one of those unicorn things – a sound without echo, black cat in a dark alley, the *Shifty* without a shadow. You're a fairy-tale, kiddo. You just disappeared. The *EYE* might have been able to trace you if she'd been in the picture back then, but *they* couldn't find you.'

Her face was unreadable in what he recognised now as her trademark neutrality.

After another pause she asked, 'What about this Krasken guy? Is he likely to waste any more time on us?'

'I don't see how he can. Where would he start?'

That unnerving pause again, then slightly accusingly, 'Maybe he has a way of contacting you.'

Stan was still relaxed though, and clearly unoffended. As always he defaulted to his slightly mocking but just inoffensive enough banter in response. 'Yep, that was plan B. If somehow he failed to kill me, and I managed to find you first as a result, I'd give him a call. That was our plan B, and you worked it out straight away.'

If he was going to stay just the right side of the banter line, she was going to balance things out by being way over on the other side of it... 'It doesn't seem like you ever had or were ever a part of any plan. What *are* you supposed to be doing here? Do you even know what this Krasken's tasked with? You don't seem to know very much at all.'

...and if she was still going to be the cold and unreadable enigma, it seemed he would still be the same indomitably good humoured all too easily readable non-enigma – balance.

He bounced back at her. 'I know I'm the only one who hasn't messed up yet. I know I'm the only one who's comfy slippers are waiting back in cosy home time.'

She blew out a quiet mock sarcastic laugh. 'Oh, ok ...but what about the, *you're supposed to be dead*, part?

Didn't you mess up by not being dead? I seriously doubt your huge yeti feet are ever going to be reunited with your big clown slippers.'

He decided to take that one on the chin and stared out of the window like he'd only just noticed they were moving. 'Where are we going anyway?'

'We are going to …a gig."

'A gig? Like a music thing? Why would we do that? You know music was a net-neg psychological and social influencer, right?'

She actually smiled at that. 'Stan, Stan, what *am* I going to do with you? It's called enter-tain-ment. Someone has to teach you how to pass as normal here. You're going to be staying a while, mister *not dead or messed up yet*. You have to get used to this place, time, whatever. Don't worry, it's not so bad …kiddo.'

. . .

He was taking it all in like an excited child. She could see again what she'd thought of as his baby face. He could never have experienced anything like this before. Hundreds of people crammed in raucous chaos, air hot with sweat and breath. People were leaning on and pushing against one another. It was a stormy ocean of excited humanity. Even without music the white noise of competing voices alone must have seemed overwhelming for him. The already low and atmospheric lighting suddenly faded to near blackness, and the ambient volume rose even higher as the crowd began to cheer and whistle. Dry ice fog spewed from the stage with brilliant points of light strobing through. Then silhouetted shadows appeared in the mist …and the roar grew even louder.

A kick drum boomed against cascading cymbals and feedback squeals. Stan watched open mouthed, like a child on a rollercoaster. The rest of the band fired to life just as something like an ancient warrior appeared out of nowhere and stormed to the front. Stan threw his arms in the air with a thousand others. His mouth was open, but the sound was lost now. Evelyn remembered *her* first gig with a strange notion of a mother duck watching its duckling. The big dope got it. She was actually quite proud of herself.

The volume dropped low enough between songs for him to shout to her, 'Let's get closer!'

She waved him on. 'You go for it, bigfoot. I'm fine where I am. It's ok …go. I'll see you later, ok.'

His yeti frame threaded forward through the sea of flesh. He was impressively agile for his size. He had an effortless way of deploying both strength and that baby face charm to carve through the crowd without offence. As he disappeared she realised just how much of a distraction he could be. She scanned the crowd again.

. . .

The following evening was a stark contrast with the previous one. Both were in more sombre and reflective moods, more so Evelyn. The atmosphere was like the feeling you get before a storm. Maybe that was what they needed; the air was always clearer after a storm. Not here though. They needed to get out for a while. Stan had already suggested it. She'd just shrugged and walked off to her room though. Five minutes later she came back with her jacket on and told him they were going out for coffee.

They quietly sat amongst the bustle and chatter of life around them. Coffee had endured into the future, but it wasn't revered with the same passion as here in *Downtime*.

What *was* though? Evelyn's mind wandered into thoughts of the enthusiasm *Downtimers* had for even the simplest things. It made their own home-time seem pale by comparison. Just looking around a coffee shop there was more atmosphere than anywhere she could remember in her own home city.

So many people crammed into small spaces here. Overcrowding had taken the blame for inflaming many of the old divisions that were studied in the future. Mostly when she was among the crowds in unfamiliar places though, she was aware only of the comparative warmth of their community. The majority of *Downtimers* were curious, inclusive …and for the most part, ever optimistic. All the horrors and insanities of history had somehow always been instigated by a miniscule minority.

Eventually the megalomaniacs, the psychopaths, the purely selfish, and all the other manipulative attention seekers, would be replaced with one unassailable authority. No human despot or self-proclaimed prophet would ever be a match for it again. It had the ability to process and cross-reference every issue everywhere in real-time, and implement global, irrefutably fair solutions with irresistible force where necessary.

Evelyn felt the familiar sense of confusing resentment. She hated that damn system, the *EYE*. It had solved most of the world's problems in pretty much a fifty-year period, only to set humanity on a course to becoming spineless zombies. She was angry too at the *Downtimers,* enjoying life all around her every day. They were growing into a new and exciting shared social consciousness, right here and now, but failing to address the abuses of the paranoid and power hungry. They were sleepwalking into oblivion. The warnings were all around, even in fiction. Their eternal optimism was blinding though.

She realised her perspective was unique. This present was the nostalgic past – a time that may have been humanity's creative pinnacle. *Her* past was actually the future – faded and colourless, but safe and preserved at least.

Between the two were all the shameful histories they learned as children. All the inescapable examples to demonstrate human inability to protect and preserve their own kind. Even to *respect* their own kind. A three-hundred-yearlong catastrophic collapse. A bloodstained rear-view mirror too thick to see through.

…Before their quantum saviour had come to slowly deliver them from the chaos. Most issues she patched within the first fifty years, but it had taken centuries to really recover.

Stan had been watching her. He found he was torn between just being *there*, and maybe trying to make some kind of connection to find out what was going on in her head. The latter won out.

'What's in your mysterious void today?' he finally asked, breaking the silence. He swirled his mug casually to catch the froth.

'What?'

'You look like you've got something kind of heavy on your mind.'

She was back with him now, back from her abstract daydreaming. 'So, maybe I have.'

'So, maybe you should talk about it,' he offered awkwardly.

'I was considering it actually.'

'What, with me? That would explain why you look so burdened.' …trying to bring some light to the shade.

She didn't look amused though, or even respond. Just seriously and serenely continued being where she was, sipping away at her coffee. Stan realised he had the same sense of disadvantage with her to the interviews he used to have with Helander. She could be quiet, as she was now. She may not be doing anything, as it appeared now. But if she wasn't doing or saying anything, she was *thinking* about it …and that made him nervous.

He tried to encourage her – as if she would need it though. 'Looking so serious makes me uncomfortable. I'm trying to figure you out still. Being honest, I think that's probably beyond me in your case, unless you help me. Sometimes I think you might want to talk about something real. I don't know whether to push or not. I know you've helped me out here, after that arrival malfunction. It's a mess for both of us. I've been more than happy so far to let you look after me while the dust settles. I don't know if I even want the dust to settle. If it's me… if I need to move on and get out of your hair now, that's fine. I am grateful for how you've been. I'm not your responsibility though. I shouldn't be your problem, Evelyn.'

She'd listened impassively and taken another sip of coffee, then placed her mug back down gently, leaving her fingers resting lightly on the handle. There was always a deliberateness and grace in even the little things she did.

She answered him quietly, 'You *are* my problem. *Everything* is my problem – you, me, this Krasken guy, the present, the future, and let's not forget every human being who'll ever live and die in-between.'

Her eyes fixed onto him again. 'I've been waiting for the dust to settle too, for five years, Stan. It's *never* going to settle. There's more dust now than a twister in Arizona… and yes, I'm still trying to work out what your *arrival malfunction* means too.'

'Ok. Now we're talking. So where are you with it all? In fact, why don't I just ask you the big question? What happened to you? Why did you disappear in the first place to be trapped in the past?'

His heart sped a little. They were way off any kind of plan, and it wasn't something he was used to. Life seemed all about improvisation now.

She seemed moody and resigned. 'Do you know what my assignment was, Stan?' The question was delivered with precision; words deliberately spaced, blue eyes holding him like a tractor beam again.

Stan braced for his lie. 'No,' he said simply.

She returned to her impassive coffee drinking, just leaving it hanging there. Had she bought it? He tried to detach his thoughts from his body so his head could spin on its own.

'Ok,' she said eventually. 'What about you? What are *you* supposed to be doing here?'

He relaxed a little. He knew this part well enough. It might not be the whole truth, but it was the truth. 'Pretty standard embedding to start with. I had a target ID to set up obviously. Not too far away, down in California. I had the extra primitive tech training. Employment wouldn't have been a problem for my skillset there. I was going after a specific AI R&D team. I had some coding to incorporate around it. Subtle stuff, but we don't get to enquire about outcomes. You know no one ever discusses anything like that with us.'

Evelyn continued to sip at her drink, casually scrolling around on a mobile phone now. 'Yes, I do know that,' she whispered.

Stan was beginning to realise that all the usual facial expressions were actually there with Evelyn. Hers was just a lot subtler than the average face. You had to watch closely, but you could definitely see those little weather changes around the eyes. Right now, her eyebrows were pulling fractionally lower and into the middle …thinking? Subtle as she might be, he was sensing tension that wasn't there a moment before. It was contagious too, as these things tend to be. He began to feel that tension. It couldn't just be their conversation. Something else was making her uneasy. His attention instinctively began to wander beyond their sphere, and Evelyn's hand spasmed involuntarily. Her mug clattered over and almost rolled off the table before she caught it, a slick of coffee and froth spreading out and spilling to the floor.

'Shass! What happened there?' He laughed, moving his leg from under the dripping table.

'Crap. I don't know. This isn't the place for this anyway. I've got some things to take care of. I need some air too. Can you go back without me, sort something out foodwise? I'll be back soon. Half hour at most.'

It was odd. Not like her to be clumsy and flustered. A little confusing, but it wasn't an unreasonable request.

'Yeah, I can do that,' he said. 'You're actually letting me out on my own? It's getting dark even. You sure you're alright?'

And now she seemed fine again. She smiled like they were regular parting friends. 'Yes. Don't get lost though, Stan. No improvised detours, ok. Not everywhere's the same here, you know that right?'

She was already heading for the door. She even gave him a small wave on her way out.

He switched tables to finish his drink. It had been a bemusing couple of minutes, but he liked the thought of a half hour of independence. On his own in the ancient city. His own man. Maybe he *should* go for a wander and take a look around. She would be pretty angry if something happened though. It wouldn't be good either. People without ID or any kind of relatable history should probably avoid awkward questions. There would be plenty of time for sightseeing later. Nice enough just to walk back alone.

He left after five minutes. Knowing her, she'd probably still get back before him. He set off in the direction of her apartment, strolling like a regular tourist, for the first time in a long time feeling something like freedom – no one to answer to, not much to do, and no hurry. Even at a leisurely tourist pace, taking in sights, sounds and smells of the old town, it would take less than fifteen minutes to get back. He was soon turning the corner to the small access alley leading to her ground floor entrance and heading for the door again.

Aware of a rushing feeling from behind, he just had time to brace himself and turn sideways on to it. A shunt from a heavy shoulder knocked him off balance. His assailant had already been reeling though, from the impact of a heavy object that had struck his own head behind the ear. The assailant quickly recovered enough to resume his attack though, thrusting at Stan's torso with a blade. The momentum of his stumble made it impossible to avoid completely. All he could do was push further backwards, throwing his balance even more. The blade hit the right side of his abdomen but pivoted over more than it travelled inward.

Evelyn arrived, spinning in backwards to drive the back of her elbow into the man's spine, her full weight and momentum behind it. It was enough to send him lurching into the wall.

Stan had been unable to stay on his feet. From the ground, he looked up to see the man turn and face her. She tried to press her advantage by driving her palm under his chin. With impressive reflexes, his heavy hand swept across to deflect it. He stepped in and grabbed her in a bear hug before spinning her and shoving her face first into the brickwork.

On his feet now, Stan charged from the side, his full weight behind a strike to the attacker's ribs. It was a bone cracking blow, but the assailant still managed to grab a hold and pull him down again. They both rolled and scrambled to their feet. Facing each other, bleeding and breathing heavily, they both assessed their options. Stan's attention switched momentarily to Evelyn, unmoving on the floor where her head had met the wall. As it did, the assailant suddenly turned and ran. Unarmed and with no advantage now, he clearly considered even odds weren't worth the risk. Stan watched as Krasken disappeared back around the corner and picked the knife up off the floor.

He realised the wet feeling on his shirt was blood and remembered the wound. Taking a second to lift his shirt and dismiss it, he went to check on Evelyn. She was up on one knee already, one hand on the floor for support, the other exploring a bloody gash across the middle of her forehead.

He put his hand on her shoulder. 'It's ok, don't get up on my account. Seriously, he just took off. No need to jump up. Take a minute.'

She took his hand and he helped her up. Blood was trickling down her face and she'd already smeared it pretty much everywhere.

He laughed at the sight. 'Oh! Check your make-up lady.'

She managed a dazed smile. 'Your friend, what happened? Where is he?'

Stan shrugged. 'It didn't go to plan, so he ran. I'm sure we'll see him again. You knew before, in the coffee shop didn't you? I knew it wasn't right …like you would ever spill coffee.'

The position of her hand on her forehead made it look like a different gesture entirely. 'Yes, I knew, and you were about to look right at him. I don't like wasting coffee, Stan. You owe me …again.'

He gave her a short nod. It was all he felt was necessary to say *Well done.* and *Good job.*

'Let's get you inside. You might want to wash up a little and re-do your make-up.'

. . .

There was no need to debate it. They were leaving. As far as Stan was concerned it had only ever been a matter of time. With the adrenaline out her system, Evelyn's default coolness was restored. Her face too, as well as Stan could manage with first aid stick on stitches. There was plenty of swelling and some interesting colour, but it sufficed as a temporary compromise between the usual impeccable façade and the recently seen blooded warrior.

'Don't worry, you still look adorable,' he told her.

She rolled her hand over and raised her middle finger. 'When I'm standing next to you I am. Aren't you going to wear your new Hawaiian shirt again today?'

He smiled and shook his head for a no. 'You ready to get going, kiddo?'

Chapter Six

They traded Evelyn's car for different unremarkable and unnoticeable model. After an hour of driving around the city in it she finally headed out south. She was quiet. Stan felt it was better to leave her to her thoughts for a while. He put the radio on to make it less awkward and stared blankly out of the window as she drove. There was no need for a big discussion about where they were going or what the plan was. She was more than capable of deciding herself. If she wanted his opinion she would ask for it.

After a tiringly tense day of driving she sent him into a small independent travel motel to book the night. When they were inside she stayed awake to let him rest first. They swapped the watch halfway through the night. He was pretty confident that it wasn't necessary, but he went along with it anyway for her sake.

The next day was more of the same. A road trip to nowhere-in-particular. She started out in a southerly direction, and then later she began to head East. By the evening Stan realised they were actually heading north again. So far they were just travelling in a big circle. He thought it might be an unconscious reluctance to leave her old home. He knew she had been happy enough with her life there. Whatever the reason, he didn't feel it was his place to question it yet. It might be something she had to work out for herself.

They pulled into another motel. This time it was a small vintage establishment. Stan thought it looked like something they'd seen recently in a horror movie. Later in the evening they drove further than seemed reasonable or practical to find a diner. Evelyn sent him in to get food to go. It was more comfortable than having to ignore the judgemental stares at her colourful swollen face and watching out for the guys sizing Stan up. By the time they stopped to eat, it was getting dark. They parked in a rest area that had a couple of wooden picnic tables set on a verge at the end.

After they had finished eating in silence, Evelyn said quietly, 'Let's go outside, get some air.'

Stan yawned, 'Yeah, that's probably a good idea. We don't need you falling asleep on the way back.'

They strolled over to the tables and sat down. It was a calm night with a gentle mild breeze... peaceful. They took their time to get comfortable and breathe in the evening air. Stan sat with his legs either side of the bench. Evelyn sat on the table-top with her legs dangling.

She made a start. 'I think I'm starting to figure this out. Whichever way I look at it though, some things just don't fit. I'm ready to take a gamble with you, Stan. I'm pretty sure I know what you're here for, but they've got things wrong before and maybe they did again. They were wrong about me, and I don't think you're really their man either. Maybe we see things differently when we're actually here, away from all the bull. We can see that we're better than that. Better than they are. We see that life can be something different. Something we had never thought of before.'

'What do you think I'm supposed to be here for?' He wasn't trying to be funny or evasive now. It was an honest question.

'The same damn thing they sent me to do. Which means this Krasken might not even be the bad guy, but the good guy who was supposed to stop both of us. If that is right, that's some pretty epically talentless recruiting. It means someone's managing to find good bad guys and bad good guys.'

'How would I know what you're supposed to be doing here?' Again, it was just a question.

She did the thing where she looked right at him with those blue lasers. 'The reason I give you the benefit of the doubt is that you are completely, one hundred percent, unable to lie, Stan. You knew who I was the second you opened your eyes at the lake. That *mythical unicorn, Shifty with no shadow* crap. No one in the *organization* discusses anything... with anyone... ever... end of story. No one knows me unless it's their business to know me. God doesn't even have that clearance. Oh, and yes, the coffee shop; another stellar Stan mess up. When I asked you directly what you knew about me you almost had a stroke.'

He looked genuinely embarrassed. 'I can't believe I thought you bought that.'

His embarrassment made her smile, almost laugh even. He shook his head and tried to smile back, still flushed.

'There it is again. Look at you, Mr big assassin.' She was shaking her head in disbelief. 'Things that don't fit alright. It makes perfect sense for me to keep you close. Easier for me to keep an eye on you and figure you out, and I think I have. But why would *you* let me. Why didn't you leave, or kill me? … and why haven't you tried to finish the job yet? Are you going to enlighten me about any of this? Or are you going to get on with all the above? What Stan?'

He took a deep breath, then let it out again slowly, trying to imagine a response that made sense. He tried to make a start, then stopped, and then tried again. 'Alright. I'm not going to make any more crap up for you to mock me with. I almost died at the lake. I know it sounds weird, but I was gone. I was over and done with all of this. What you were saying about seeing things differently, you can't have a much more different perspective than death. I felt it. I *really* felt… the only thing left of this world was you. You didn't save my life Eve, you pulled me back from death. The first thing I saw after that was your face. Let's just say you made an impression, like looking at an angel or something. I was Krasken's priority but sooner or later he would have gone looking for you. No way I was going to let that happen. I thought if I stayed with you, I could look after you. You could look after me. We could let some of that dust settle for a while. Maybe we could even get our heads around this mess.'

Evelyn nodded and shrugged her shoulders. It felt like progress. 'Ok, let's see if we can build on that. I don't think you're lying this time. It's possibly the only thing you ever got right… obviously I am an angel.' She considered fluttering her eyes but thought better of it. 'Might we go a step further then? Let's say, I'm not going to kill you, and I hope you're not going to kill me.'

'You haven't so far. I haven't so far. Where there's life, there's hope, right?'

'Hope is ok. I was hoping for more than hope though. Try, I am definitely, categorically, not remotely, ever, considering murder as an option… ever.'

Stan was as earnest as she had ever seen him now.

He was actually giving *her* the look as he obliged with the requested affirmation. 'If anything happens to you, it will be because I failed, not because I succeeded... and I'll already be dead.'

She didn't have a reply for that. She looked at the floor, pressed her lips together in something that might have been a small smile and just nodded a little.

. . .

The next morning, they were back on the road again. There was no doubting the subtle change in atmosphere between them. Both were going through their mental adjustments and figuring out what it meant. It would take another long drive in silence for either to be ready to face a discussion about the future though.

It was wild country. A weather front had ushered in a deep low pressure and the rain whipped against the windshield on angry gusts. The low sky was a swirling mass of different greys now, from darker gunmetals to the occasional brighter shades where the pale violet sunlight managed to sneak through. Gnarly pines rocked away on both sides as the winds strengthened. Eventually the road snaked down to the edge of a long lake. Evelyn pulled their car into a lay-by overlooking the shore and switched off the engine.

'It must be different,' she said. 'The *EYE* must be running things now, obviously. I'm just trying to picture how that works. How do things turn out like this with her in charge? Are McAndre and Helander still involved even? I can't imagine human minds being allowed to influence outcomes anymore.'

Stan patiently tried to explain. 'You're half wrong and half right. When you say the *EYE* is running things, she's kind of not. Mac still runs the show, or at least he believes he does. He doesn't *know* about her involvement. She knows everything about him and mostly leaves him to it. Maybe she just monitors things and only interferes when it suits her, like with me for instance. She knew what was supposed to happen, and it wasn't in her plans. Instead of going through Mac though, she came directly to me. She ordered me to go along with it until I got here, then just forget it. She effectively modified my assignment to a five-year vacation. Coding only.'

Evelyn watched the raindrops merge into streams on the glass. Confused, she asked, 'Why the deception with McAndre?'

Stan shrugged. 'Don't know. She always has a plan though. I do know that much. An NHI doesn't leave a human mind in charge of anything without a good reason. I have thought about it, but it's been out of my mind while I've been here.'

The glass was coated in a sheet of water that flowed down in waves now.

'Did she discuss anything strategic with you? Do we even know what Mac's trying to achieve by taking this guy out?'

He thought about it, shaking his head. 'Not much, no. He, maybe a descendant even, is responsible for some causality that impacts the *EYE* in some way. That's all I know. How about you?'

She huffed. 'Less specific than that even. Neutralise a future threat… all very dramatic.'

Stan raised his eyebrows at her with a lip-pressed smile. 'Whatever he's supposed to be responsible for, the *EYE* clearly isn't as convinced as Mac about how they should deal with it. How did you find out about the *EYE* being involved anyway? I got the impression I was the first one in on that secret.'

She had known already, of course. Even if she hadn't, she would easily have gathered as much by now from Stan's frequent slips. She decided it wasn't necessary to mention that. She had come to see his carelessness more as endearing than a fault.

'Because I was the one that let *her* in on the secret, just before leaving for my *shift*. I had the *five-year vacation, come back and it will be sorted* speech too.'

Stan was genuinely surprised. 'Really? How? Why? When?'

'A couple of days before I was due to leave. Things were nagging me too much. Nothing felt right. The excuses for the *EYE* not being involved. Our deletion from SIS. How we were ever supposed to come back from the dead if *she* doesn't know about it? The fact that we never heard from or met anyone from a previous *shift*. Surely, we could have benefited from their experiences. A brief seminar or something.' She paused looking distant, thinking back. 'I always liked Janeen. She looked after me more than she needed to. I was fascinated by all the mind stuff, and I wanted to learn from her. I was always asking about it. Occasionally she'd tell me something, and it felt like she was passing on some mystical mojo. Now you think *I'm* nuts. Anyway, I think I knew her pretty well, and she was definitely off about something at the end. Something wasn't right, and it was something she couldn't just come out with. One thing I learned from her... you don't necessarily have to speak to say something. Nothing was ever accidental with her. It was all design.'

She moved her neck around, stretching out the tension. '*Shifty's* don't come back from the dead, Stan. Never have and never will. Maybe they make it out of the water, but I'm sure enough they don't make it back to the city.'

His anger made a rare appearance, 'You believe that? Nobody? Ever?'

'Stan, Stan. I know they kept us busy, but didn't it ever cross your mind? As far as Mac was concerned, the *EYE* could never discover the loop. He thought it would be too dangerous, that the extra dimension of infinite possibilities might blow its mind and de-stabilise society. This whole thing does have massive implications. We get so caught up in the training and bullshass that we forget how mind blowingly massive it all is. If we're allowed back to a normal life there's a risk that one of us will blab something. We're loose ends, and they're too careful to leave us blowing around. It's not worth the risk. How would *EYE* time go after five years anyway? – *Hi! Long time, no see. Been anywhere nice while you were apparently dead?* And how would our fellow citizen-kind take it?'

'I amaze myself sometimes, I really do. I don't claim to be a genius, but I didn't think I was an idiot. You say it just like that and it makes instant perfect sense.'

She released her seatbelt and kicked the door open.

'Where are you going?' he asked.

'Even angels need to pee.' She screwed her face up against the damp gusts and set off for the trees, hair flapping madly behind her. Stan decided it would be wise not waste the opportunity and made for his own tree. They both arrived back at the car puffing against the cold wind and rubbing their hands.

'That was refreshing,' he griped. 'Good call, Eve. Excellent rest stop. I definitely rate the facilities here.'

'Always the whining with you. Tell me what we do now, Stan.' She fell quiet, with a look that meant it was a serious question and she wanted a serious answer.

'We find Krasken.' He said it without hesitation.

'Ok,' curious. 'What makes you say that, or even think it's a possibility?'

'I don't know. I'm just putting it out there. If you want answers he's the one most likely to have them. He's the only other source there is here.'

'So… finding him?'

He thought for a minute. Nonchalantly he eventually answered, 'We just go back. He'll find us.'

She did her little side to side head-rocking, thinking and weighing thing. 'Ok, let's do that then. It's worth a shot. Probably what he hopes we'll do. It's the only place we all have in common. He should be keeping an occasional eye on it at least. It actually makes some kind of sense… kiddo.'

They drove away from the lay-by with the foundations of a risky plan, feeling more positive at least now that they had one. *Shifty's* enjoy nothing more than the focus of a defined challenge. It would be a quiet drive back to the motel though as they considered the details and the risks. If Krasken was around, there was the small matter of how to avoid being murdered by him.

Stan was the first to break the silence again. 'We go back, not to the apartment but to a hotel or something. You return to your work at the museum as usual. It's a good area for surveillance. He'll pick up your trail… and hopefully I'll pick up his. He'll want to track you back to where you're staying. I can track him, tracking you. He won't try anything until he knows where both of us are.'

She nodded, 'I'm bait. I like it. Does he even know I work at the museum though? And are you good enough to do this without him finding you first?'

Stan rolled his eyes. 'Come on, Eve. He is an A hole, but he must have scoped you at work before. Call it plan A if you like, just in case he is that incompetent and we have to think up another... and don't ever worry about me.'

She shook her head and smiled. It soon faded into seriousness again though. 'You need to be alert, Stan. This is a no second chances situation. Someone rates him. He tracked us back to Seattle, and I thought we were being careful enough then. We need to be crystal clear about this. When, where, and how. Precise. We need to be mobile too. We need to get a van.'

'A van? Fine. But just like that? How are funds? I never ask, but you keep paying for everything. You can't earn that much.'

She started to play around with her phone again looking almost a little coy and shrugged. 'I had five years with not a lot to do. I'm sure you were trained along similar lines to me. I had a feeling something like this might come up one day. Don't worry, I have enough. I'll let you know when it's a problem. I'll sell a kidney if I have to, one of yours. I don't think either of us needs a retirement plan, do you?'

He shrugged too. 'Thanks for pointing that out. Not something I'd thought much about yet, so yeah, thank you.'

She shrugged back at him. 'There's a little town south of the city. We can stay there tomorrow and do our shopping. I'll get in touch with work and tell them I'm back in on Monday... and you're welcome, you know I'll keep you real... kiddo.'

Chapter Seven

Krasken almost coughed out his breakfast. It had only been a week and a half. Could he be that lucky? Could she be that stupid? He was eighty percent sure he would never see either of them again. But here she was, Medi-dress across her forehead, shades on. Tidy job too, even without the make-up. The suit and shoes helped. She must have called in sick with a bullshass story about a fall and an emergency room visit. It would give her an excuse to disappear for a while. The sensible option would be to disappear for good and never look back. Maybe she hoped he would assume that. She had a bloody nerve though.

He snapped out of his happy daydreaming, angry for watching her as long as he had. *Where was the blonde oaf?* It was possible they had separated. The smart thing was to be anywhere but here. Maybe he had moved on alone.

He scanned the road nervously, triumph giving way to feeling exposed and vulnerable. He needed to be cool and take his time now, check every detail on the block. He'd been having breakfast in a bagel shop, one of a handful of hideouts with views up to the Klondike, when she had literally strolled right across the frontage. It was only a small place, not somewhere he could wait all morning. He couldn't just get up and leave right away either though.

He started to work on his exit. It was possible the blonde idiot was lurking somewhere. He could track the little black-haired bitch later. He needed to know she was alone first before he took care of her. At least she had had the sense not to go back home.

. . .

Her phone vibrated in her suit trouser pocket. She answered it against work policy in the public area of the museum and listened to the voice.

'We've got him, Eve. We should do this right away while we can. Before he has time to think about it and get creative. It's safe for you to leave now. Get to the car and stay on the road. I'll keep you updated with the location. I'm thinking we might pick him up around the college kind of area. Hopefully we'll get him in the back with some *gentle persuasion*. If I have to throw him in the trunk things are likely to get tricky and sticky though. We'll need to get to the van and out of here as soon as possible.'

'Got it, Stan. On my way. Do you want to keep this line open, or shall I call when I'm on the road?'

'I'll call you back when you're mobile. Just stay somewhere around Squire Park for starters.'

. . .

At the parking garage she blipped the car and slid into the back seat, casually checking her phone again. Inside she opened a bag containing among other things a change of clothes. The business suit and heels were swapped for track pants, a zip hoody, and a well-worn pair of Asics. She pulled her hair through the back of a Seahawks cap in a high ponytail and took a deep breath. It was time for a clear head now, to focus on the task. No room for distractions now it had begun.

Out of the back, into the front – ignition, shift, move. Flowing. Graceful. Precise. She fixed the Bluetooth smoothly on her left ear.

The phone lit up – *Stan*. She answered before the tone even started. 'Ok, we're open for business. No messing around, Stan. Just give me info, brief and clear.'

'Got it. East Thomas near 18th, on foot, heading west. Having a bit of a lull at the moment. He looks more relaxed now. Might be about done. Once he sees me though anything could happen, so finger on the trigger. If it blows up, I'll stun him. Don't try and help with the lifting, ok. Just cover me and deal with anything and everything else until he's in.'

'Ok, I've got you, Stan. Four minutes to your location. I'll close in and time it right.'

. . .

She could see Krasken walking north on 15th, opposite side of the road. She drove past him from behind. The barber shop sign was only a hundred and fifty yards further ahead.

'Just passed him, outside now. He's almost here. Twenty seconds…five, four, three…'

Stan stepped out of the doorway directly into Krasken's path. Only eight feet separated them. The gun muzzle was clearly visible under the jacket on his arm.

He spoke evenly and clearly. 'Ride's behind you Krasken, or it can end here. You've got three seconds to work it out. Ride or bleed. Quickly now, before I choose for you.'

Evelyn had already glided out of and around the car, casually opening the back door like a chauffeur. She looked completely relaxed like she might be waiting for a chihuahua to jump in. There were people on the street but there was nothing to see so far.

Stan's heart pounded as he held Krasken's wild stare. He'd stopped dead, body rigid as he weighed his options.

Evelyn's calm voice came from behind him, casually counting down. 'Three seconds, Krasken... three... two...'

He held his arms away from his body in a subtle gesture of compliance and turned to the open door.

'Right side please, and don't forget to buckle in.' She sounded pleasant and professional, as a museum guide should.

Stan followed him into the car with the jacket and gun. Three seconds later Evelyn was back in the driving seat. Her own weapon appeared in the space between the seats while Stan settled in next to Krasken.

'Smooth and steady,' she advised. 'To be clear Krasken, we have no real expectation of cooperation so there'll be no hesitation to finish this early if needs be.

As soon as Stan was comfortable she faced forward and pulled the car back into the early afternoon traffic.

· · ·

They left the city with Krasken secured in a tub chair in the back of the van. On the road, Stan would stay in the back too. They agreed that Evelyn should handle the interview. Stan was happy to leave it well alone in the meantime. He had no desire to converse with the man who had tried to murder him twice already anyway.

They drove to a remote forest access track for the privacy they needed. It was going to be unpleasant any way you looked at it… not much above freezing, damp, and a relentless biting wind. They both knew it was better if Stan was out of the way, just not *too* far out of the way. They picked up a tent and some supplies so that he could be outside and there, without actually being *there*. It was never going to be much more than tolerable for any of them, so no point dragging things out longer than necessary. Krasken would either cooperate or be worthless – worthless and dangerous. Evelyn intended to make it clear from the outset that expectations were limited and not a lot of time would be wasted.

Stan set his shelter up away from the van so Evelyn could get straight to work. There wasn't much he could do to keep warm. He couldn't even walk around without being a distraction. After he'd been out of sight for long enough, Evelyn got out of the front and moved into the back through the side door. She sat on a bench seat opposite Krasken, relaxed, scrolling on her phone, looking almost like she might be waiting for a bus.

Without even looking up she made a start… 'We don't feel any animosity towards you Krasken, you know that don't you? You were given a job to do, and we just happen to be that job. We have no right to judge you. Obviously it makes sense for us to deal with the threat though. Difficult to move on if we don't. You understand that too, I know you do.'

Krasken sneered back, 'Don't patronise me. I might have failed, but I'm not an idiot. I have no desire to drag this shass out either. I assume you went to the trouble of keeping me alive for a reason. What are you so desperate to know? Just ask me, then I can say no, and you can get straight to the fun part. Sooner you ask, sooner you get started, sooner I'm dead.'

She continued casually, unphased by his reaction. 'No, there won't be any torture however this goes. It's not my style, Krasken.' She was flicking around on her phone, occasionally looking like she'd seen something interesting. 'I'm curious. Have you ever killed anyone before? I mean before all of this, before here and now in *Downtime*. I saw most of what happened at the lake obviously. Stan filled me in on details about the bodies ...the wounds. Seemed like overkill. Don't you think? We definitely thought so.'

'What if I have,' he growled. 'You want to label me a psych risk, how twenty-nine of you. But it's not exactly breaking news is it. We don't go unnoticed in twenty-nine. We're taken out of circulation before we even know why ...so accidents don't happen. Looks like we still have our uses though.'

She attempted to sound dispassionately compassionate, and actually felt like she might have pulled it off. 'You're right, it's not breaking news, and of course you can be useful. I want to hear your story, Krasken. I'm genuinely interested in your perspective. It's too easy to be judgemental, like it's too easy for shassholes to take advantage of you. That's the real shameful part. They picked you out for what you are and played you. I can relate to that much at least.'

Krasken chuckled, humourless and mocking. 'You can relate? Course you can relate, little Miss Therapy. I think I might be having an epiphany. I feel better already, and so liberated. Thank you. Can I go?'

'What do you think of this place, Krasken? I mean in the twenty-ninth there are no opportunities like there are here. It must have occurred to you that life could be so much better. It's a crazy world. It could be fill-your-boots crazy. I won't pretend I'm not trying to put ideas in your head. I am. Life has to be easier here. A lot more fun than *Point*. Maybe somebody already suggested that? Did they even want you to go back?'

Krasken was grinning and nodding. Maybe she could reach him after all.

'You're a clever lady. They warned me you were.'

She turned on her collaborative tone. 'Well *they* are not wrong. I am a clever lady. I have plans and ambitions of my own believe it or not - mostly involving sticking it to the idiots responsible for sending you after us. You have your plan, and I have mine. In the grand scheme of things, we're a minor part of your plan now. We were just a means to an end, surely.'

She finally set her phone down next to her on the bench, still very casual and relaxed. 'I only have one card to play Krasken, and this is it. If you can tell me anything I don't already know, anything that might help me understand what's been going on, maybe I'll let you get back to your twenty-first century crazy life. It would be your chance to live a little. Believe me, you would never see us again.'

He was shaking his head though. 'Trouble is, I know you won't do that. You still think like a twenty-niner. I'm a risk to society even if I'm not a risk to you, right?'

With the purest sincerity she answered, 'It's not something I'm comfortable with either way. You might be dangerous, but like you said, you're not stupid. Stan and I can do things that might outweigh any damage you do. I'm not like you, Krasken, you know that. I don't have your issues. I don't like to hurt people. I certainly don't like the idea of having to kill you. I'm an honourable person. If I give my word, it means something… and I *will* keep it.'

He looked down at the floor, thoughtful, calculating and balancing the options he had left. 'What do you even want to know that would make a difference anyway?'

She shrugged. 'Which side are you actually playing on for a start? Are you team Mac, or with the *EYE*?'

'*EYE* calls the shots. Always has, always will. How could you think it could be any other way?'

'Alright, I thought so. Just confirming it. So your orders were – kill all the *Shifty's* and you don't ever have to go back. Is that right?'

'Very good. What did you need to speak to me for?'

'The lake then,' she pressed. 'Let's talk about that. The first two you killed, it was pretty quick, if a little unnecessarily messy as we mentioned before – they never had a chance. You dealt with those on land though. With Stan, you went back into the water. That seems risky. It evens the odds a bit doesn't it?'

He smiled slyly. '...especially if he had some help. Answer to the question you already know is – yes, we were hoping you would show at the lake. Apparently you're strong in the water. Perhaps you'd be tempted to intervene. *EYE's* idea, second gen smart. She thought that if you *were* alive you might be curious enough to have a look at the new *shift*. You're a loose end and part of the deal. It was a perfect opportunity to have everything over and done with on day one. Might have been the only opportunity.'

Evelyn nodded; she suspected as much. 'Ok. Janeen Helander. What did she know? Was she even aware of the *EYE's* involvement? Did she know what you were going to do?'

He still wore that sly smile. 'Oh dear. Are you sure you want to ask about momma Janeen? The dutiful little bitch servant of the *EYE*? She knew what the job was. She handpicked me to do it.'

71

Evelyn looked down at the floor. She nodded acceptingly and looked up again. 'Alright Krasken, just one last thing, I think. What's with this guy that McAndre's so intent on murdering? Do *you* know who he is? Do you know what Mac's trying to achieve?'

'I know what he's trying to achieve. McAndre thinks big. He's a humanist. He wants to rid us of meddling AI. Not only that though, somewhere along the line he had a crazy notion about righting what he sees as a great historical injustice. He could prevent the first assault that kicked everything off. He could save what would amount to tens of billions of lives over the three hundred dark years. Obviously the *EYE* could never let that happen. However the twenty-ninth came about, it worked out alright for her – manageable population, security, sustainable quality of life, resources, and environment. I don't give a rock who your mark is. It's above my pay grade. Isn't that what they say here? The *EYE* was probably worried I'd kill him too if I knew.'

It didn't feel quite right, but it did make a kind of crazy sense. 'Surely if McAndre changed the past to that extent he wouldn't even exist anymore, never mind be who he is, doing what he does.'

'He's an idealist. A fundamentalist. Maybe he just doesn't care about that. These humanists would sacrifice themselves for a future without AI in a heartbeat. They might have a point too. If it wasn't for the *EYE*, we'd still have Jack Daniels and cigarettes.'

'I've never even heard of a *humanist* before. Is that a real thing?'

'Enough of a thing to be a concern for the *EYE*, especially when they can re-write history and the future. Without that possibility they would be nothing. It's not exactly easy to advertise and recruit in the twenty-ninth. I can't see there being a massive social revolution under the all-seeing *EYE,* can you?.'

Evelyn pursed her lips as she thought. Not really thinking in words – more a subconscious settling and processing of information, making space for new ideas without pre-judgement. It was her way. It always had been.

'You've been more than reasonable, Krasken. I need to get out of here for a while. I need some space to think about all of this. I'll talk to Stan afterwards and we'll see where we are. If there's nothing else, we might think about cutting you loose.'

'What about your new best bud? No questions about him?' he asked.

She shook her head as if it was a stupid oversight on her part, then realised it actually was. 'Of course. Stan. What can you tell me?'

'Probably nothing earth shattering. You're smart enough. You've spent time with him. He was originally recruited to be a straight up old fashioned *Shifty.* Strange thing is though, he wasn't Helander's recommendation for the *big job.* Mac decided all by himself that Stan should be his man. Why would he do that?'

'I don't know. I suppose at the end of the day, Janeen advises him. He doesn't have to take her advice. What do you think, Krasken? Enlighten me.'

'I think Stan was kind of sympathetic to their cause. Maybe General Manipulating idiot somehow realised that. My guess is that he nurtured that attitude in Stan. Maybe he thought that if Stan believed they were doing the right thing, Stan *would* do the right thing... eventually. The *EYE* made it clear to me she wanted both of you dead. Out of the two though, he was the priority. Probably because you already demonstrated you haven't got the balls for it. Do you see?'

'I do see, yes, thank you. Like I said Krasken, I'm going to take some time with this. We'll talk again soon.' She got up to leave and then paused in the doorway. '*Momma Janeen* hand-picked you to do a job – a job you failed at. I've never known her to be wrong about anything before. I'm not a hundred percent sure she was this time either.'

She jumped out and walked back to the front of the van. Instead of getting in, she leant against the door for a moment with her head tilted back and her eyes closed. She took a few deep breaths, hoping the cold air would blow some of the fog from her head.

After a couple of minutes, she walked over to Stan's shelter. 'Wakey wakey, big foot. Go sort him out. Let him do what he needs to do and secure him again. Then we'll talk.'

'Yes Ma'am, will do. I was just getting comfy here too.'

. . .

'Well?' Stan asked. 'How did it go? Or how is it going?' He had a feeling she had a lot to talk about, not necessarily all good, and was wondering where to start.

'I don't know,' she answered quietly. 'He's talkative enough though. Ironically, he probably feels more relaxed here with us than he ever did in his life before – even considering what we may or may not do with him.'

'Ok, so? Anything interesting, useable …or believable?'

He was trying to move her along gently. She was in a preoccupied state of mind; there would be no rushing her.

'He's confirmed a few things I think we already knew. I think I know who's on who's team sheet. We discussed the motivations of various people we know. That's the interesting stuff, if it's to be believed... and I think I do. Not a long story, but maybe it brings a slightly different perspective into focus.'

'Looks like he made an impression. You seem a shade darker since your conversation. Might just be my imagination.'

She wasn't about to comment on her emotional state or views just yet. Especially when he seemed to be fishing for them. She had some fishing of her own to do first.

'He spoke about humanists. Not something I've come across before. How about you?'

Stan had been expecting this at some point. Like it or not, it was coming sooner rather than later. 'Yes, I've heard of it, or them.' He stalled, weighing up how much to offer what the reaction it might bring. 'What did he have to say about it?'

'In a nutshell, it's the motivation and driving force behind everything McAndre does.' Then she added with a subtle interrogatory look, 'Krasken is under the impression that you might have some sympathies along those lines yourself. He suggested it might have been the reason Mac chose you to finish the job they gave me.'

'Ok. It's something we spoke about. I'm not going to lie to you about it, Eve. I thought they made some convincing arguments. Especially in light of what the echo loop offers us now.'

'Like the chance to go back and murder people we don't agree with?'

'That sounds like the kind of emotive language politicians here use. When you know the reality of an outcome, it's not so simple to say it's absolutely wrong to kill one individual.'

'It's wrong. See how simple that was? The outcome? What outcome are you talking about exactly, Stan? What are you hoping for in *your* ideal world? What is it that this poor unsuspecting guy needs to lay down his life for? Enlighten me if you even know. No one bothered to fill *me* in on any of this bullshass before I left, before they packed me off to snuff out some kid. I was supposed to just follow orders… like a good little *Shifty* would. I wasn't important enough to know about the greater good.'

Stan felt irritation, frustration, and general confusion suddenly taking over his life. They had been drawn into this conversation at precisely the wrong time… before *he'd* even figured it out. He had imagined working this out together over time, with space to let things settle. Instead the little sable haired cannon was firing on him like he was the arch enemy of all humanity. He took a five second count to breathe deep and regain his composure.

'E, …'

'Don't bloody *E* me.'

'…we have a lot to work out. I knew that anyway, and so did you. We've been taking one thing at a time so far. Taking Krasken has brought everything to the fore at once. We can't expect to get our heads around everything right now. Why don't we just concentrate on our immediate situation first.'

Evelyn, always impeccably calm and composed, was actually glaring at him now. The unhealed scar across her forehead was doing nothing to soften the effect. She still managed to keep her voice even though. 'Right, yes. What about that? I think we're done here – so what about that, Stan?'

'Are we even going to be able to discuss this? I get the impression you don't want to take responsibility for anything at the moment. Do you want me to make the decision… so all you have to do is be angry?'

She turned her back on him for minute, then turned around again. 'Shass… I want to let him go, Stan. I know every reason why we shouldn't. I'm not happy about it. It's just what we have to do. I don't think he'll get in *our* way again. He has issues and he will be a problem for someone else at some point in his life. The world's full of assholes. We can't be responsible for all of them.'

Stan nodded gravely. If giving Krasken up could keep them together while they worked things out, it was a trade he could live with.

Evelyn relaxed a little. 'I know it's not ideal. He tried to kill us. He's tried to kill you twice. I'm pretty sure given the opportunity, he'd try again.'

'What about us? Are we still riding on the same wagon?' he asked her.

'I think so, for now. I'm not sure we're both heading for the same destination. What about you? … because you need to understand something, I'm really not cool with all this killing people.'

He let finally his breath go, along with some of the tension. 'You don't need to ask. I already told you, you don't need to worry about me. It is different when you're here. I'm not so sure about anything as I used to be. Definitely there are things we need to work out at some point. I still think we can do that.'

They stood quietly. It wasn't an uncomfortable silence, more of a subliminal continuation to a quiet resolving. The quietness of the place was astounding. It demanded attention. It was almost a feature in itself, as real as the trees or the ground. It subtly framed all the other sensory information – the cold, the moisture in the air, leafless branches clacking in the wind, creaking trunks…

fleeting mists of breath… hair blowing over an eye… heartbeats.

Evelyn eventually broke the silence. 'Does this sound like a stupid idea? It's something in my head. I might even have dreamt it, just to give it some real credibility.'

She paused, waiting for encouragement. Stan shrugged for her to carry on.

'Those two that helped us at the lake…' She could see the cogs turning in Stan's mind too. 'They already knew something was different or special about the lake. The old guy said as much… and they were there. So – people who know there's something special about the lake, happen to be there at exactly the right time. How much do we believe in coincidences?'

Stan felt goose bumps rising beneath his hair. 'How the… how did we not think about that for one second? Or even at any time since.'

'I know, it's not crazy is it. It's crazy we're only thinking about it now. You know, we're trained not to hang around that area. We had our drama. You had your near-death thing. Krasken was an unknown. I think we overlooked the significance because we just wanted to get out of there as quickly as possible.'

'We have no idea what they know, or how they know it. We could have just asked, and they probably would have told us. No way of finding them now.'

Evelyn looked like the kid in the class who knew the answer. 'There just might be, Watson. They mentioned a Res. It's a short form for reservation. I think they're descended from a native people. There are places that were set aside and protected. They obviously know the area well. They must be fairly local. We know their names.'

'So we look for them? Go backwards to go forwards? Who's Watson?'

'Sherlock Holmes? Doesn't matter, never mind that. Yes, go back to go forward... unless you had *other plans*?'

The look she gave him left him in no doubt about the meaning of *other plans*... and it implied strong disapproval.

Chapter Eight

They drove all the way to Portland to unload Krasken. He had no money, no transport, and no ID. His life would be complicated for a while. Even with the strongest will, he should be inconvenienced long enough for them to untraceably disappear.

As far as Krasken would be aware, they were making a fresh start – travelling in any direction, any length of time, settling …who could guess where? Anywhere on the planet for all he knew. They would be completely off grid, at least for days, maybe even weeks on the road – until they would be far enough away to make it highly unlikely anyone could ever pick up their trail. There would be no motels, no busy café rest stops, no obvious stopovers at all. They would be fully gassed, probably with extra in cans. They would cover bear miles quickly without stopping to talk to anyone.

What they would actually be doing though, was driving East through Oregon and Idaho, before looping back to Washington State.

Krasken might stick around to see what Portland had to offer, if he was in no hurry. They both guessed he might eventually head south to California though. Why not? It rained less at least, and there would be plenty of options for establishing a life there.

Evelyn did her best on the journey to research the native peoples and reservations of the northwest. She had a gut feeling about one in particular, claiming a kind of logo badge on a website seemed familiar. Maybe something she'd seen on one of them at the lake, on a bag or jacket perhaps.

Many of the previous *Shifty's* had passed through Seattle on their way to wherever their assignments took them. Evelyn though, having abandoned all hope of ever returning to *Point*, decided she liked it enough to settle. She'd lived all of her *Downtime* life there and made it her home. The native people associated with the image she thought she'd seen before, were the Sauk-Suiattle. The familiar look of the words alone made it seem as good a possibility as any. Stan had nothing to compete with woman's intuition. If nothing else, it would be a pleasant journey.

They set right out after dropping Krasken, covering a few hundred fast highway miles before using the little roads to get really lost. Their mood had lightened a little. They had purpose and direction again …and their old nemesis was just a fading nightmare now.

· · ·

Two days into their roundabout road trip they pulled into a gas station just a little way north of Darrington. It wasn't clear if it was open or not, so they parked up. There was no sign of anyone.

'Wait here. I'll see if there's someone we can talk to. I think it's better if I do the talking,' Evelyn said, kicking her door open.

'What's wrong with me doing the talking?'

'Just wait here alright. I wonder if they have a bathroom for customers.'

She walked over to the square brick building and disappeared through a door. She'd only been out of sight for about thirty seconds when there was a tap on Stan's window.

'Hey there. Need any help?'

Stan lowered his window. 'Hi. Yeah, my friend just went inside to find you. We were going to fill up. She might be using your bathroom if you have one.'

The man was probably late fifties and reminded him a little of lake man. He had a quiet confident way about him too.

He smiled, friendly. 'No problem. You go right ahead and help yourself when you're ready. I'll see you inside. Still got a way to go buddy?'

Stan saw his opportunity for glory. 'Not so far now. We're pretty much where we want to be. We're here to see a friend. Well, a friend of my …girlfriend. Maybe you know her? Taya?'

'Taya? I know a Taya. Might even be the same one. I never heard of anyone else with that name.'

The glory was definitely calling. 'That's great. That's *really* great. This is going to sound a bit strange, but we don't know exactly where she lives. Eve lost her address. Any chance you could point us in the right direction?'

'Nope.'

'No? I know it sounds a bit weird, but it's not weird. Ok… it is, but it's not.' The glory was starting to fade.

'It is, and it's not. Ok.' He looked more amused than concerned. 'Look I know a guy. I can give him a call if you like and see what he says. See if he thinks it's *weird*, or *not weird*. How does that sound? Who's asking again? Eve and…?'

'Stan. That would be cool. Stan and Evelyn.'

He strolled away and disappeared through the same door Evelyn had. A couple of minutes passed before she reappeared. She opened the van door and climbed in the drivers' seat.

She casually checked her scar in the rear-view before speaking. 'So, anyway, apparently we are weird… and yet also *not* weird – and you wonder why *I* wanted to do the talking – because you always have your bigfoots big foot in your bigfoot mouth.'

'He knows them. He's going to call them, smartass. So remind me why you do the talking again.'

'He might call them. Or he might just call the local strange police. In which case our lack of any relatable past will make for an awkward evening's accommodation in a local station. Let's hope the right people show.'

Twenty-five minutes later, a dusty hardtop jeep pulled in. The station guy came out to meet it and spoke to its occupants through the driver's window. After a couple of minutes, he went back inside. The jeep then drove over and parked next to their van. They had already identified the familiar faces from five weeks ago inside. *Only five weeks*, thought Evelyn. It felt like half her life in *Downtime* already.

Older guy, or Raymond as they would know him from now on, had a stony poker face. Taya though was smiling and waving like they were old friends. In the van, Evelyn had the poker face, Stan was smiling and waving. Evelyn looked at him and shook her head.

Raymond got out first and walked over to Stan's window. 'Nice to see you again. I didn't think it would take you this long.'

'You know how it is. Time flies when you're keeping busy. Nice to see you too,' Stan replied.

'Will you follow us? You might as well stay at our place tonight, and it might seem *weird* talking through car windows in a gas station.'

Evelyn looked at Stan and shook her head again. 'Is it far?' she asked. It was the longest sentence Raymond had ever heard her speak.

'Should take all of about five minutes in this traffic.'

There wasn't any traffic. Stan was happy to let Evelyn to do the talking now. She had ground to make up with these two in that respect.

'Ok, lead the way,' she said. 'We'll be right behind you.'

She was making a rare effort to sound sociable. Stan gave her a thumbs up and winked as she put the van in gear and pulled away after them, still shaking her head.

· · ·

Their house was a simple wooden cabin all on one level. A decent size though, and uncluttered. Stan liked it a lot, a house he would live in too. Organic, practical, and unfussy. Most of their things were functional, and the few things that weren't were loved pieces of artwork.

'This is a really nice place,' he commented. 'A really nice place, *in* a really nice place.'

Evelyn copied his example. He was her role model for friendly and sociable. 'Yes, it is. It's …beautiful.'

'Thanks,' Taya beamed. 'A lot of history here, right Raymond. This place and the whole area.'

'Yes.' Raymond nodded. 'You're welcome to stay tonight. We have plenty of food if you haven't eaten. Better to eat and rest before thinking about other things. I don't think there's any need to rush, is there?'

Evelyn looked to Stan for an answer. She was surprisingly unsure and out of her element in someone else's domestic situation. In business, even in combat, she had unfailing confidence and self-control – but this was totally different – relaxed, homely, like family... *alien*.

He rescued her. 'That's really generous, thank you. If you're ok with that, that would be fantastic. We'll try not to be in your way too long.'

Raymond just nodded. Taya was obviously more than happy with it, and asked Evelyn if she would help in the kitchen. Stan was sure Eve swallowed nervously as she followed her. He was happy enough to be left with Raymond though. He had a paternal aura about him. There was no doubt he was an honest, rock-solid good guy. Not overly talkative, but comfortable to be around.

'Thanks again, Ray. I don't know if we even said that before at the lake. We've caused you enough trouble already I know, but we'll keep disruption to a minimum now, I promise.'

'We have nothing more important to be doing right now – and we'll tolerate as much disruption and inconvenience as we need to. No need to worry about us.'

'Yes, we will I guess.' Stan found himself nodding too. 'I don't know if that principal stretches to Eve being in someone else's kitchen though.'

Finally Raymond smiled, and things were really feeling alright. They did spend the night there, and the next.

· · ·

On their fifth day at the cabin, after a simple afternoon meal of fried fish with boiled vegetables and homemade bread, Evelyn made excuses to get Stan out for a walk. It was less than two miles along a wooded trail to the river where the fish had been caught. It was so beautiful and accessible that it was already becoming a routine. It was a convenient way to give everyone their space too …and a good place to talk.

'Stan…' she began.

'What?'

'Why are we here? Why are we interested? What are we hoping to achieve?'

He frowned and shook his head. 'Why do you bombard me with questions like that? You don't say anything for three hours while you go over things in *your* head, and then you expect me to be on the same page.'

'I don't know. I'm giving you options. Start where you like.'

They walked on, quiet again, thinking.

Stan finally came up with an answer. 'We are here to find out what they know, and how they know it. We want to know, so we can add that to what we *already* know, so then we can decide what, if anything, we are going to do about it. How does that sound?'

'Or what you could say is, we're deciding whether or not we should finish what we came to do in the first place. Isn't that right? If it is, don't we already know enough to make that decision?'

Stan tried not to sigh. 'Alright Eve let's do this. Try seeing it from a different angle. To you the choice is about one person, right? Does he live, or does he die? You want a definitive answer. It's either wrong, or it's right.'

'Right, it's wrong,' she shot back instantly.

'Ok, it's *wrong*. So, now you have about ten billion people. Human beings. They are all going to die. A lot more will suffer horrendously. You could save them. Do you save them, which you have the power to do, or do you leave them to that fate?'

She shook her head. 'No Stan, that's something completely different. That happened. It happened naturally. It has nothing to do with us.'

'It hasn't happened, Eve, and it has everything to do with us. We are here, now, before it happens. We have advance knowledge, so we have a choice whether we like it or not. Deny it or don't, do something or do nothing, kill him, don't kill him, save them, don't save them. These are all *our* choices. They're my choices, and they're your choices. Naturally is just a word. Whatever we decide, it will always be *natural*. As unappealing as it might seem, the whole see-saw future pivots on us right now. There's never been this degree of consequence resting on the actions of two individuals. This isn't about *The Organization*, or Mac, or the *EYE* anymore. It's just you and me.'

Evelyn felt stiff with the cold, or tension. 'How so? We're from the future. If we do nothing it will still be there. Things will just continue on as normal.'

'Normal is just a word too… and how much longer are things going to be *normal* anyway? People don't make their own decisions anymore. We don't control anything. We don't invent or discover anything. We don't make anything. We don't really even make ourselves anymore. Human beings are declining, and that damned machine has us wrapped up so we can't do anything about it.' He stopped walking, standing with an expression she hadn't seen before. 'Don't think this doesn't hack me off too, Eve. I didn't know what we were signing up for either. Whatever we do now, history is going to judge us one way or another.'

Evelyn leant against a tree, head back, looking up through the branches. 'I can't get my head round that. If God needed a break, he wouldn't leave us in charge. I was a surplus kid. It's miracle enough I wasn't terminated as a child. I don't imagine they were saving me for this.'

'Well, you're not surplus now, and if I was picking someone for the job, I could do worse than pick you. You're a good person, Eve. If you can't figure this out, don't worry, we were screwed anyway. You could be wrong about one thing though – maybe you were saved *precisely* for this.'

She breathed the cold air in and blew out a long stream of mist. 'Come on, let's get back. Time to see what they know. See if we can work this out. We can at least agree we have plenty of time though, until the next potential. We don't need to rush into anything.'

. . .

They made their way slowly. Partly because they were still processing their conversation, and partly apprehensive about the potentially even more confusing information Raymond and Taya might add. Perhaps something else slowed their progress too; Stan realised that he didn't exactly find her company unpleasant.

The late afternoon sky had been dimming for a while and it was fading quickly towards darkness. With the sun behind the hills, the temperature was dropping even lower. Evelyn seemed to keep bumping his elbow as they walked side by side. He half expected, half hoped maybe, she might thread her arm through his ...probably not though, life was complicated enough. Even if it hadn't been, he had no reason to believe she thought of him in that way. If he was honest, he wasn't sure she had *any* reasons to like him at all. They might be as far apart as it was possible to be.

Krasken stepped out casually from behind a wide trunk, not twelve yards ahead of them. They stopped dead in surreal automatic response. He was just waiting, looking confident and smug, hands buried in the pockets of a long trench coat.

See how impressed they are. Look at their faces. You can see the realisation and fear dawning. You can see them struggle for control against the surging adrenaline already. They won't dare move now.

He wondered who would speak first... *Will it be Stan, bold idiot protector? Or Evelyn, the bitch counsellor? Does she still think she has a rapport? Will they know their place; speak when spoken to? Surely, they'll wait. I'm in charge here. I'm the power.*

They were *all* waiting, silent and frozen. It seemed like forever.

Too excited to wait any longer, Krasken broke the silence. 'You go your way. We go our way. We never see each other again.' He said it with triumphant sarcastic satisfaction. He knew his lines. He'd seen this moment in his mind already. 'Twice you underestimated me. Twice you got lucky. You think I would let you go on thinki...'

She'd been standing too close to Stan, too relaxed, too distracted. Her gun was in the back of her pants waistband just under her jacket, on her left side, the side where Stan was. Her right arm became a blur as she pivoted backwards, arcing behind Stan as the gun came out, right hand only slowing to allow the left to deal with the catch. Then two loud cracks ...and a deeper, louder percussion before they faded. The two rounds buried themselves in

Krasken's torso. He reeled against the impacts, trying to bring his own weapon on target. Two more loud cracks were followed by another booming reply. Krasken staggered backwards, still on his feet but with his gun arm hanging slackly now, grip failing. There would be no more return fire. She stepped forward relentlessly as he fell backwards, tracking him all the way down. Her aim adjusted upward to his head as it came to rest against a tree root. One last round split into his temple and she held her stance while the silence returned. It was over.

She turned to Stan as if startled awake. He was on the ground, flat on his back. He was conscious but starting to writhe as the agonising pain really began to register. She checked for the wound. It wasn't so obvious at first with his dark coloured wool coat. To look at him, the pain was coming from everywhere. She found it on the right side, almost where the collar bone met the shoulder. It looked like it had grazed under the bone and gone through.

'Roll onto this side. I need to see the back.'

He didn't speak, just grimaced and nodded. He tried to help as she stood over him and pulled him up by his coat. He lay with his legs stiffly straight out as she checked the back.

'It's out Stan, ok. It's out. It might not be too bad. There's not a load of blood here. There would be a lot more if it hit something bad.'

He nodded, feverish and dazed, 'It bloody kills.' He grunted and writhed some more. 'You might have to think about getting out of here.'

'Be quiet. Hold on, ok. I'm calling Raymond.'

Stan crawled to the base of a tree and dragged himself to an upright sitting position. He was grinding his teeth, trying to get to grips with the pain. Evelyn's voice on the phone was a noise he couldn't focus on or make sense of. He looked at the lifeless Krasken, slumped with bloody head lolling unnaturally. He felt sick, drained, and spinning. He could easily imagine himself that way right now.

Evelyn considered trying to drag Krasken off the path a little and covering him with twigs and leaves. He was too big, she was too small, it would take too long, and Stan still needed attention, even though she didn't believe it was immediately life threatening. She put her hands front and back of his wound, holding pressure from both sides.

'We better hope Ray gets here before anyone else comes along. Shass... I'm sorry Stan... I had to.'

'Course you did. You're... quicker, and I'm... a big lump of cover. He was always going to hit one of us. You timed it... just right, kiddo. Relieved you did what you had to.' He groaned again, rolling his eyes. 'If it gets... complicated, you need to get out of here. Not an easy way out, Eve. One of us needs to stay in this. Should be you anyway.'

'Don't worry, I will if I have to. Take it easy, bigfoot. This isn't exactly a tourist route and it's going to be fully dark soon, and it's bloody freezing. It might just work out. Probably going to be a DIY job on you though.'

He was shivering and looked frozen, partly with the cold, mostly with the shock. She resisted the urge to hug him for warmth. It was more important to keep pressure on the wound. It wasn't all that far to the cabin. Ray and Taya shouldn't be long.

It probably took less than twenty minutes. The last light was already disappearing. Taya arrived first with a rucksack full of bandages and torches. Raymond was a minute or two behind her. By the time he was on the scene, they already had his coat off and were bandaging him up. It was starting to look like mummification, under his armpit, over his shoulder, across his body to the other shoulder and armpit. They put his coat back on over his shoulders. Raymond helped him with a hat and some gloves.

'Alright. All you need to do is stay on your feet. We brought the van as far as we could up the track. It's not too far. Just lean on these two and go steady. You're going to be alright. I'll take care of this mess …again.'

Stan tried to thank him, 'Ray…' but the pain flared making him nauseas.

'Not now. Help these two to help you.'

He shuffled slowly, concentrating on the ground, leaning heavily on Evelyn and Taya who were under each arm. They encouraged him quietly and constantly to keep him calm – and distract him from thoughts of how far he had to go. Eventually the long freezing shuffle in the dark brought them to the van. His breathing was laboured, and in the torchlight he looked ghostly. They both helped him into the passenger side. Taya climbed in after him as Evelyn jumped in the drivers' side. They were all relieved to have made it so far …but it was going to be a long night.

Chapter Nine

They heard the door open and three sets of footsteps on the creaking wood floor. Raymond walked ahead of the two distressed looking visitors to show them out. No one spoke as they left. The door banged closed behind them and a discussion took place outside. After a couple of minutes, Raymond returned alone rubbing the fatigue from his face. Taya and Evelyn waited until he seemed ready.

'Is he ok, Raymond?' Evelyn asked quietly. 'Can we see him?'

'He should be in the long run. They patched and sedated him. He'll be comfortable enough for now. Is everything else ok? I don't know; it's a lot to ask. I'd rather not ask favours like this. Joan's a good person. She works out of the Darrington medical centre. She looks after a few people around here. I'm pretty sure this is the first bullet wound anyone asked her to fix though.'

'Do you think she'll report it? What did she say?' Taya asked.

He sighed, 'They're good people, Tay. She knows she's involved in something she shouldn't be …and she won't want to explain the things she does for other people around here either. We talked about whether she could help. I said we'd understand if she couldn't.'

'Well, I'm grateful she did,' Evelyn said. 'I would have liked to tell her myself.'

'Maybe another time. They've had enough for one night. *I've* had enough.' He turned aimlessly, like he couldn't decide where to go or what to do next. 'Go see him. We'll leave him to you for now. He won't know you're there for a while. And there's no hurry, Evelyn. You're going to be here for some time and that's fine.'

She nodded, relieved. Stan wasn't going to be fit to move anywhere in the near future. 'Thank you, Raymond; and thank you too, Taya. I'm really sorry you're having to deal with all this again. I'll see you in the morning.' She knew as she walked to their room that Stan was the only one who would get any sleep that night.

With Evelyn gone, Raymond spoke to Taya. 'It will be better if you talk to her when the time is right. You know all I know. Tell her everything. Answer her questions. Tell her about Whitehorse and Silver Lake. You'll be fine, Taya. You know the way now.'

'Alright. When do you think?'

He shrugged. 'A few days? A week or two? Let this settle first. Stan will be fully occupied with his recovery for a good while yet, could be months.'

. . .

Raymond had been up and out early before it was even light outside. Taya was last to rise as usual. The door to the kitchen was closed but the smell of a cooked breakfast was wafting through the whole cabin. She decided to see if she could scavenge some for herself. 'Mmm, smells nice. Morning Eve. Is all of this for Stan?'

'Yeah, you want something too? It's just light veggie stuff. Meat free sausage, beans, mushrooms, but I'm scrambling some eggs. You'll have to put more toast on. He never eats much first thing anyway.'

'I can live with that.'

Breakfast sorted; Taya's attention turned to the main business of her day. 'Raymond won't be out long. We could go somewhere – drive, a bit of a walk, some fresh air. Stan will be fine for a while. It's going to be nice out. It'll do us both good.'

Evelyn continued cooking as she considered the offer – *Motive? How long for? Will Stan be ok? Will I be ok? Can I be bothered? Am I going crazy in here?*

'Yeah ok, why not? I don't want to go too far though,' she finally answered.

'That's fine, just a couple of hours or so.'

Evelyn nodded and smiled at her. 'Best check he's still alive first. I'll see you in a little while when Raymond gets back.' She picked up the tray and left for Stan's room.

'Alright bigfoot, time to start filling that hole in.'

He *was* alive, propped up on pillows. 'I don't know. I feel like crap.'

'Don't whine because you got shot. It's harder for me. I have cabin fever. At this rate we'll still be here next winter. They haven't adopted us, Stan. Have something to eat. It's like sharing a room with an animated garden gnome. Why do you wear that stupid hat in bed anyway?'

'It's cold.'

'No, it isn't. It's too hot.'

'I got shot you idiot. It hurts …a lot. I'm cold. Where the hail did you train to be a nurse?'

'I'm no nurse, kiddo. Take the hat off, eat, and start looking a lot less gnomic …or I'll shoot you myself and put you out of *my* misery.'

He could almost have laughed, if he *could* laugh. *Maybe I can try something after all*, he thought. He forked the scrambled egg into his mouth. A few more mouthfuls and he was actually starting to feel better, and almost hungry, as good as things got lately.

'Raymond's back soon, and he might be even less nursey than me. We're a lot of what a senior citizen doesn't need in his life – patching bullet holes and clearing bodies after us.'

'Lucky for me you're in charge of nurse duties then.'

'I'm going out – Taya's idea. She's probably been delegated with the business of …whatever the business is. Maybe she'll fill me in on what they want us to know, and I'll try and find out anything they *don't* want us to know.'

'How's our situation here? All your mocking aside, I'm really not ready for the road yet. Better to be here a while if that's possible.'

'I think we're ok. That's what they keep telling me.'

He seemed relieved, and tired …really tired. 'Let's not mess anything else up then. We need to make the most of their hospitality as far as I'm concerned. We ought to be on good terms when we leave too.'

'We are, and we will be Stan, don't worry about it. I'm going to leave you for a while now. Get some rest. You ok?'

'Yeah, I'll be ok. Are *you* ok?'

She rolled her eyes, 'Why ask if I'm ok? *You* got shot,' and then just left.

. . .

Taya drove south, through Darrington and out the other side again. A short while after they turned up a narrow track, wild looking forest thickening around them as they climbed. She pulled the jeep onto a small grassy clearing about half-way up. Evelyn hopped out and looked around. She spotted a small foot trail crossing the track just ahead, continuing up through the trees to the right.

'We walking now, up there?'

Taya was settling a bag on her shoulders. 'Yup, that's it, onward and upward.'

'Not too far I hope. It's pretty wild up here.'

'It opens up ahead. You get a view then. It's worth it, don't worry about that. You see the old world there. The way it's been for long time. Hopefully, the way it will a long time after we're gone.'

They were both quiet as they walked up the moderately strenuous trail. Taya had been right about the weather; it *was* beautiful – light breeze, high wisps of white cotton cloud, plenty of blue sky. Not cold either, especially walking the incline. Evelyn wanted to move things along though. She hadn't come for sight-seeing.

'Come on, Taya. Let's get on with this. Don't be shy with it now.'

'I know. I was wondering how to start, how to do this. It isn't something I've spoken of with anyone else, just Raymond.'

"Alright,' Evelyn said. 'I'll ask questions if you like, you just answer. If you feel like elaborating, just go for it.'

Taya nodded, still looking unsure.

'Ok, the most obvious point is that you know there's something special about *that* lake. So ...do you know exactly *what* is special about it?'

Taya was full of nervous tension, clearly feeling pressure to get this right. As she started to explain it sounded over-thought and clumsy. 'It's like, a doorway. People come here from another place.' She hesitated, '…like you. You must know this. You must have come from that other place.'

'Ok. So, what do you know about this *other* place?'

'It's kind of, this place …but different. The place is the same, but different people live there, like another dimension I guess. I've heard of it being described as different things – mirror world, serpent realm, echo lands. Are any right?'

'They're all *kind* of right.'

That gave her a little more confidence.

'Obviously *we* don't go there. There are people around this area that have known for a long time. We watched people come and go for a long time. We kept the secret, and we watched.'

Evelyn frowned. 'When you say *we*, who is *we*? And how long are we talking about?'

'We. Us. Raymond, me, some others, and people before us. People of the rivers who live between the mountains, from the Redface to the Whitehorse. How long? I don't think anyone knows exactly. A long time I think. Generations. People were not always as concerned with measuring time as they are now …and other things have happened of course. How would we know now?'

Evelyn shook her head, bemused. "So, you are saying you, and only you …your people, are the ones who know? It's your secret? …Wow Taya, how many people are we talking about? How many right now?'

'Twelve. Six here in the south-west. Six more further north and east. Always twelve who know and watch.

A few elders who passed it on and don't concern themselves anymore.'

Evelyn watched her with a look of slightly impressed wonder as she started to grow more confident and tell the story. She and Raymond were special. They must have been *chosen* to carry on a tradition that appeared to have been going on for generations. It was like a mysterious calling. Clearly it was a big deal to them.

Taya walked on in silence again. It seemed a deliberate space for Evelyn to digest and consider what she'd heard so far, which she did.

'Taya, *why* do you watch? Why haven't you or anyone before revealed this big secret to the world. You could have been famous, and rich too with this story.'

'It's something too important …isn't it? You should know. People get things wrong. They always do. These doorways have a purpose. It's something magical …there are stories and prophecies about them.'

'Do you believe *we* are magical, Stan and me? Now that you know us?'

She looked like she might have goose bumps under her hair. Just the look on her face was enough of an answer. She did speak though, quietly, almost breathlessly. 'Yes, I do.'

'Taya…'

'No Evelyn. Talk about anything else if you like. I believe, and Raymond believes, that you have an important destiny. I wasn't sure at first, but I am now. I know you don't know what it is yet, and I can't help you with that. Don't waste your time telling me we're wrong and it isn't true though. You are the two who are *different*. *You* killed the serpent of the lake. You will help both worlds, yours and ours.'

Evelyn was lost for words. It seemed ridiculous, but ironically it could almost be true. Taya's story resonated with Stan's speech on the day Krasken had appeared from nowhere. The day *she* had killed him. Could anyone really believe that some universal power had conspired to put any kind of fate on *their* shoulders though?

They continued on, up through the forest, Evelyn's concerns about being out too long forgotten. It seemed the perfect place now to be free of distractions, perfect for considering new realities. Ahead the trees began to thin, forest giving way to a rocky plateau, and the trail disappeared. Taya made her way across it to a natural stepped formation on the other side. The plateau, enclosed by the rocky steps and the forest, and surrounded with icy peaks in every direction, was almost like an amphitheatre. The place had serious atmosphere. A circle of stones or an ancient monument wouldn't have looked out of place. There was nothing though. No trace of humanity at all, ancient or modern. It was just a pristine arena of nature.

Taya sat herself down on one of the large rock steps and Evelyn sat next to her. As they rested quietly in the fresh mountain breeze, the cogs meshed again in Evelyn's mind.

'You said the doorways had a purpose, right?'

'Yes, we believe that.'

'By doorways, you mean the lake, where we came from?'

Taya shrugged. 'Yes.'

"But you said *doorways*. Plural?'

'Do you only know the one where we met?'

'Yes! I most definitely do only know of the one where we met. If you're telling me there's another somewhere that is very big news to me. Where? How many?'

'Three. The lake you know. One right over there,' she pointed towards a middle-distance peak. 'at the foot of the Whitehorse mountain …and another much further north and east – Silver lake is hard to reach at the best of times.'

'And people come through these too?'

'Not for a long time. *We* haven't seen anyone. I don't know of anyone who has.'

'So why do you think they are doorways?' Her excitement was starting to fade.

'It's knowledge that was passed to me, like it was passed to the person who passed it to me. I don't know who the first was, or when that was. Like I said, people haven't always been so obsessed with measuring time. They *were* doorways, so they probably still *are* doorways.' Taya delivered it as a universally accepted truth. Evelyn had a feeling that questioning the authenticity of the original source might cause irreparable offence. She waited respectfully for Taya to continue. 'My grandfather brought me here. Right here, where we are now. This is the place where he first told me the stories about the lakes. About the people like you. One day I'll pass them on to someone else. When I do, it will be here. This is where Raymond learned them as a young man. This is where we all hear them, even the people from uprivers. The rocks here know the stories, they help us understand.'

How much factual truth was in the stories, Evelyn couldn't guess; but she did understand that Taya believed in every word. It seemed more important to respect that than to question the evidence. 'I want you to know something, Taya. I have no reason to doubt anything you've told me. It's a real privilege for me too, to witness that kind of integrity and dedication. Some people possibly still think your ancestors were less worldly and wise than their own, but *your* ancestors discovered something incredible. What really impresses me is that they didn't try to destroy it or use it. They didn't try to profit from it. What they did was accept it, respect it, and protect it. I think… it's awesome! I really do. *You* are awesome, Taya. All the stuff I've seen and done, I think you beat it all… and the implications… what it could mean…'

She struggled herself with that. What *could* it mean?

'…I thought we had two choices. I don't care much for either. I'm not sure yet, but this might change everything.'

Already she was feeling energised about the possibilities taking shape. Taya's information had given her a new perspective. Instead of plan A and plan B, she was starting to believe in the possibility of a plan C. Maybe it was this place. Maybe the rocks were helping her to understand. Things were hardly ever exactly as they seemed.

Chapter Ten

Stan wondered if he'd ever be able to get back to his old self. It frustrated the hell out of him. He was getting nowhere. If he was improving, it was so slow you wouldn't even notice. And he wasn't just down, he was at the point of real depression. The lack of activity was affecting his brain. Surviving mentally could end up being his biggest challenge yet.

There was *some* cause for optimism. He was eating a little better, he was managing short walks around the outside of the cabin… and at least it was an excuse to keep all the other stuff on hold for a while.

That other stuff was always there though, just below the surface, as dark as those thoughts could be. It always came back to haunting numbers for him – billions versus one …or maybe even two …every now and again that thought would torment him as well. What if Evelyn…? What happens if…? He could never reach the obvious conclusion.

The subject was on hold. Sometimes he tried to talk, and she'd listen, always noncommittal and neutral, maybe having mixed feelings about his progress or lack of any too.

Taya was doing a good job of keeping her occupied. They walked a lot. They would go into town. They were even fishing together. It had been an opportunity for Evelyn to work on her fitness too. With not much else to do, she was probably in her best shape since leaving *Point*. For all the time she spent with Taya though, she didn't seem to have discovered anything that they couldn't have guessed anyway: the unusual activity at the lake had been noticed, they still didn't know by who, or even when exactly. It had been observed, but not interfered with. It had become a blend of local mythology and tradition.

At least she'd stayed though, and her concern for him seemed genuine enough. She made an effort to help and encourage him, she talked about *Downtime* stuff like they were *Downtimers*, she even made an effort to make him laugh from time to time – humour seemed to be a recent development in her life. He hadn't died, and she hadn't left. Where there's life, there's hope; where there's a will, there's usually a way. They would find the way. They'd work it out …he hoped.

. . .

Evelyn had been up early and gone out. He'd heard her on the other bed, shuffling about, getting ready for something. Early fishing trip maybe? Too dark and cold for his liking yet. He rolled over and went back to sleep.

. . .

It was after six. Taya and Evelyn had been gone all day. Stan resolved not to show any undue concern. If Raymond was concerned, he would mention it. If he didn't mention it, there was nothing to be concerned about. They were sitting in front of the TV when they eventually heard the kicking off of muddy boots out on the porch. Another minute of shuffling passed. The outer door creaked open and banged shut again. No voices though. Raymond still didn't seem to think there was anything odd about their silent return.

Taya walked in without meeting their eyes... alone. Raymond didn't look at her either. He was looking at something that looked like nothing in a corner of the room. The sick last to know feeling started to rise in Stan's stomach as the silence continued for agonisingly long seconds.

He almost felt too weak to ask. 'Hey, Taya. Everything alright? Where's Eve?'

She looked at Raymond, who was determined to look anywhere else for as long as possible.

Eventually he did speak. 'Evelyn has had to go. She was afraid to concern you with this right now because you're still recovering.'

Stan fought to control his breathing. It almost felt like a panic attack – not for worry of what she might be doing, just because she was gone. It was something he hadn't felt before. The feeling of betrayal had taken him by surprise, and it showed. Taya and Raymond were there to witness it too, making it even more intense. Even aware of it he couldn't hide it. He felt childish. Why would anyone want to involve a stupid *child* in their plan anyway?

'Ok. I guess I should have seen that coming. I should get out of your hair too. I didn't intend to be here so long...'

Taya shook her head and interrupted. 'I tried asking her to wait. She intends to come back. She hopes you'll stay here with us, at least 'til you're fully recovered. We hope you will too. We want you to stay Stan.'

'Why *would* she? We don't come in pairs. It's fine. We were never a team, Taya. Evelyn's been alone all her life. That's why they choose us in the first place, for our emotional detachment – born alone, grow up alone, train to work and live alone …die alone.'

'That might have been true before. It isn't now. You *are* a team. We're all a team.'

'Yeah, so what's our team member doing? Where is she? What couldn't wait, or even be discussed with *the team*?' He was struggling to keep emotion out of his voice.

'She wanted to see if there might be another way. Something that neither of you had thought of yet. Not just for her, something hopefully you can both believe in. A better way for us all I think. She asked me to trust her …and she needs *you* to trust her, Stan.'

'This doesn't feel much like trust. Trust works both ways. Does it look like she trusts me?'

Raymond had been quiet up to now, but he broke in before Taya had chance to reply. 'This is the time to be confused, time to be upset, time to lash out like an angry child.' He could command authority when he chose to. Sometimes it was clear you had to listen. 'Tomorrow will be the time to understand. The only thing you need to hear today is that Evelyn *does* trust you. If she didn't, perhaps you would be lying in the ground next to the other one. Maybe we would too. Taya has a note. Read it. Sleep on it. Then tomorrow, be quiet for a while and listen.' He stood then and left the room.

Stan and Taya respectfully held the silence. As the moment passed, she walked to the drawers and came back with an envelope.

She tried to smile as she held it out. 'Yeah, what he said, definitely.'

She sat down next to him, both staring at the made-up dramas playing out on the muted TV. '*I* don't know, but she said you'd know what this meant. The choice is still there, and it's still yours to make. She's taking nothing away from you. She just hopes you'll wait. Sounds to me like she has a *hell* of a lot of faith in you. Sounds like she *really* trusts you.'

He tore open the envelope shaking his head and pulled out Evelyn's handwritten note.

Bigfoot. I know this is a shock. I know you're not going to be happy about it. The fact is, you're injured. You would never accept it, but you're not up to this right now. I know you would try and postpone this so you could go too. I don't think it's a good idea for both of us to go anyway. You staying here keeps all of our options open. I found out from Taya that there's another portal. I have no idea if it works the same way, or if it's on the same loop. If you're reading this I might be back in Point, in some other time, dead, or on another planet for all I know. I'm asking you to wait and see. You have all the time in the world, Stan. At least give it until the next shift change. If it is open season on Shifties, the fact that you are here might be leverage to keep me alive. Taya can tell you everything, just not at 'the place'. I hope I can explain that to you later.

Eve

. . .

He'd read, and he'd slept too. He knew already what Raymond had meant when he told him to listen. It's exactly what Evelyn would do – clear the mind, let things settle, arrive at an understanding. He had …and now that he had, he hoped he hadn't taken too long. It was time to send his own message.

No more.
Look after time girl.
If I don't see her soon.
EYE will see no more.
Stan Xx

The records of certain publications had survived all the way into *Point Time*. They were used as a message board for *Shifty's* to 'check in' and report their status. The word '*EYE*' capitalised, flagged the message. The *Shifty's* name in the appropriate monitored time frame confirmed that it actually was a message.

No more LIES. I see her again, or you *won't* see again. Shouldn't be too subtle for an advanced Artificial Intelligence to understand. He was in a position to pull the plug, and there was nothing anyone could do about it from *Point*. His message should be enough to verify Evelyn's bargaining chip and strengthen her position with the *EYE*. He was slightly concerned that the message would also herald her arrival. Unlikely she would be able to re-enter the city and that society unnoticed anyway though. Recognition systems were routinely operational everywhere. There were so many different forms embedded in the fabric of everyday life – for maintenance, for efficiency, for safety, for convenience, for education, for comfort, or in one word – control. The *EYE* was the omnipresent witness of all human life. Evelyn couldn't just assume an identity as she'd been trained to do here, and without a valid identity she could have nothing – nowhere to stay, no access to meals, and no means to travel. It was impossible to fake an ID in *Point*. You were monitored and recorded from birth. You were your own constantly updated biodata: fingers, hands, ears, eyes, breath, DNA, face, voice, medical history, micro-biology. Only you could be you, and you could only be yourself.

He caught himself reminiscing on her resilience in the face of unfavourable odds. She'd never been hesitant or unsure. He remembered the lake incident as he first arrived in *Downtime*; literally diving straight in to rescue a complete stranger, and Krasken's crude assassination attempt in Seattle; crashing in from nowhere like a cannon ball to save him again... and then when Krasken had reappeared; she'd done what she had to. Under pressure she was infallible. People seemed to sense her calm and confidence authority, and usually had the good sense not to challenge it.

He thought about her returning to *Point*. Metaphorically speaking, she'd just walk right up to the front door. If they didn't open it, she'd knock it down, five feet seven and all of her. He just wished she didn't have to do it alone.

· · ·

Evelyn was through. Whenever and wherever she was, it was much colder than when she'd left – the translucent glow above her was ice, which luckily wasn't too thick yet. She was prepared though, determined and well equipped. Taya had helped with the sourcing and transporting the gear she needed. No need to hold her breath, freezing in her underwear this time. She was suited up, with cylinder air, and had high tech winter clothing for later stored in a dry bag. Most appropriately right now, she also had an ice axe.

As she emerged from the broken ice at the edge of the lake she was satisfied right away that it was the right location at least, and it was *much* colder as she hoped it would be. Where she'd started in *Downtime* it was unseasonably mild. The area should be colder in *Point Time* because of the future/historical climate balancing measures. The peaks and high ground were blanketed in thick snow and around the lake there was a covering of about four inches. A few flakes were still fluttering on the breeze, but the sky was bright enough. The most recent fall must have all but blown out.

She dried and changed before setting up her shelter on the shore. There was no sense trying to cover any more ground today. She'd travelled up from the cabin in the morning, swam her way through a full cylinder in the water trying to locate the portal, then spent twenty minutes of intense exertion just breaking through the ice. It made no sense getting even more fatigued before anything had even begun.

There was another reason to take her time too. She was sure, hoped at least, that Stan would send some kind of message ahead. It was a calculated risk to allow him to do that on his own initiative. If she'd asked, or told him, it would seem like she'd assumed command, and he would feel their partnership was unequal. He was going to be sore enough already about being left behind. *He* needed to do something. He needed to feel they were still a team.

It was going to be a long and cold first night out. She was completely at ease with that. In fact, she was looking forward to it. There was pretty much zero chance of encountering any other human life in this place and time. No influences or distractions – no better place, and no better way to reset and recentre herself, and that was something she needed to do before going back. She needed to re-affirm her place in the world and time. She could do that here, among the mountains, trees, rocks, and frozen lakes, under the stars in the dark winter sky. She could retune her senses as an out of context observer, just listening to the wind humming through the restless bare branches and following the gusts as they rumbled down the valley.

It occurred to her that although she knew *where* she was, there was no way to know for sure yet *when* it was. For all she knew it could be a hundred years before her birth, or ten thousand years in the future. Why not? What difference did it make in this place? Apart from the weather it was always the same. The peaks were formed millions of years ago. Life came, and left, and came back again, time after time. *What a feeling, to be free of time. The time is just now.* Her last semi-conscious thoughts as she faded into peaceful sleep were of the stars, and the timescales of galaxies …the unfathomable vastness of eternity.

She awoke in the morning still with that feeling of utter freedom, refreshed and at peace. For now, she didn't even need to worry about food. The surreal nature of the current situation wasn't lost on her; sitting on a rock, looking out over a frozen lake, displaced in time, eating a packed lunch her friend had made. She could, for all she knew, be the only human being on the planet at this moment – eating a sandwich.

She was going to have to make a move though. It seemed a long time since she'd received any training and instruction on survival in the wilderness – she was not an expert! At this time of year, it was obviously a good idea to stick to lower ground. Her rations wouldn't last indefinitely, beans, lentils, nuts, dried fruit etc. Not things she would find in these parts, and she didn't relish the prospect of having to catch, cook, and eat meat.

Another thing on her mind was how to find her way through to the north-western habitat area - the city - Neam. It was located roughly between where Seattle and Portland used to be, just a little further inland. Although she was definitely in the right place, even accounting for the different weather, the landscape was different too. The woodland was denser and wilder. The area was totally unmanaged now. The trail she had taken before with Taya didn't exist here. Assuming this was *Point Time*, it was going be heavy going to get back to civilisation. It would be wilderness all the way to the outer recreation band, the managed natural habitat zone that represented the outer most limits of the city.

Further in from those outer managed wild areas were the agricultural bands of crops and livestock. Those circular bands around the core accounted for twenty-five miles of the total radius. Inside those were the main recreation band with its emphasis on parks, gardens, physical activities, and controlled wildlife viewing, anything that passed as outdoor leisure in an AI controlled world. Once through the inner rec you arrived at the high status residentials, a band of individual dwelling estates, each surrounded by their own land for personal use. Beyond that, surrounding the core, was the general residential band, home to ninety-five percent of the city's population, made up of blocks of societal accommodation in a variety of external sizes, shapes and heights, but all with standardised interiors in one of four levels appropriate to one's status.

The centrepiece of the city, the *core*, was an enormous plex and steel dome over a vast excavated crater in the earth. Inside were seven enormous mezzanines, four below and three above ground level. Surrounding their outer edges were all the social, artistic, culinary and supply outlets, the central spacious hubs of each being variously purposed public spaces.

Carving through the whole western radius of the city's bands, and flanked by all the administrative and infrastructure buildings, was the *Mainway*. A dead straight arterial laneway running from the *core* to the outer limit where it became the *Interway*.

It would be possible for her to enter the city from any direction. There were no significant barriers around the wild outer zone. Agricultural areas were protected from larger wildlife with charged field fencing, but there were plenty of unattended gateways. The city wasn't a fortress. There was no enemy outside. Once through those gateways accessways of the farming areas all eventually connected to the inner rec and the residential zones. It was her intention to walk right up to the front door though, metaphorically speaking. She would enter from the west and walk the *Mainway* as far as possible, before being inevitably detained. One way or another it was the most direct route to authority. It made *sense* to be direct, there was nowhere to hide anyway.

With everything packed she was ready to go. She walked back to the rock she had claimed for a last look back over the frozen lake. Across its corner, some variety of wild cat looked back at her from its own rock. It wasn't huge, but it was probably considering things that wild predators tend to consider. They watched each other for a while, both calm enough, neither seeming particularly threatened or desperately hungry. Evelyn decided on a policy of full disclosure anyway. She unclipped her sidearm, waving it above her head with one hand while pointing at it with the other. The cat continued to watch her, unmoved and unimpressed. She bent down to pick up a good-sized throwing stone and launched it in its general direction. It made an unnatural clacking noise as it landed on the ice two thirds of the way across. Still the cat seemed unimpressed. It casually lowered its head, pushing its curious nose out towards the stone on the ice. She picked up another. This time she threw it along the shore to clatter on the rocks. The cat might have raised an eyebrow but was determined to hold its ground.

'Really? Do I look like a rabbit to you?' She levelled the handgun and managed to hit the rocks a dozen yards from where it was. As it made a hasty retreat she shouted after it, 'Yes, you better run. I didn't come back to take shass from anybody. Not from cats, not from bears, and not machines either. You better stay out of my way, 'cos I won't give you the benefit of any doubt. I will *cook* you. I will eat *you*!' She was smiling as she returned to pick up her backpack. 'Have you missed me twenty-nine?'

And with that, she was on her way.

· · ·

She found a place to settle in the outer wild rec band. A slight hollow in the side of a hill with a small oval of level ground. The side where she set up camp had a good view over the landscape falling away below. Over the ridge on the other side was the *Mainway*, running all the way to the domed core that was just visible on the horizon. While her rations lasted, and the weather held, it would be comfortable enough. She needed to allow enough time for the *EYE* to pick up on Stan's message, *if* he had sent one. If there was no message, it would still be more comfortable than a detention cell.

It was getting to the point though where justifying further delay was starting to feel like cold feet. She looked out of her shelter on the wintery nightscape rolling away into the distance, snowy hills lit softly by a half moon. The starry sky was alive with silent streaks of space dust vaporising in the atmosphere, a myriad fiery ends to their incomprehensible journeys. In times gone by people would have taken such a celestial display as an omen, a sign from the gods. Perhaps it *would* turn out to be premonitory and symbolic of her own fate. The decision was made then – tomorrow she would be in the city.

Something seemed amiss though. She was aware of a growing feeling of unease. Her senses were reaching and searching. Had there been an out of place sound? Was her unconscious mind questioning something her eyes had passed over? Or was it just general tension over what tomorrow might bring?

There it was again. A soft scuffing from above and behind her shelter. Night creatures in the wild were not so careless. She resented the fact her journey would end on the *EYE's* terms now. It would have been nice to enjoy one last night and arrive by her own will.

Wide awake and with heart beating hard, she called out to the darkness. 'I'm sure you must be armed, like I'm sure you must have orders not to use them. Make no mistake, I have no such reservations. You will show yourselves on the hill below me. I urge you to be sensible and civilised.'

It seemed the longest wait in silence. Then came more obvious dragging and scuffling sounds before a voice called down; a woman's voice that carried authority, even in its compliance. 'We will do as you ask. We are coming around. I advise you too to be sensible and civilised.'

Evelyn responded assertively, determined to command respect and impose some authority of her own. 'You know who you are dealing with. Make sure I see all of you, I don't want anyone to be shy now. And light this place up, there's no need to sneak around in the dark.'

As she emerged from her shelter, four torch beams were already swaying down from above. She was aware of other unlit figures at her flanks making their way downwards too, the closest only a dozen yards away. Then without warning the whole hillside exploded in brilliant floodlight from the ridge.

Chapter Eleven

There were half a dozen figures in front of and below her, and a few more waiting above still, possibly another half dozen. One of the ones below, presumably the woman who had spoken, stood alone between her and the rest of group.

Evelyn noticed the groups striking non-uniformity straight away. She'd expected to see a unit in *SecCore* standard issue. Teams selected by the *EYE* were not just uniformly equipped, they tended to be similar in appearance even. This lot were an assortment of shapes, colours, and sizes – ages even – some probably too old to be field active. The woman in front of her was well into her fifties. She was an imposing character though. Her skin was dark, physique lithe and strong, her posture confident and upright, eyes challenging and intelligent; Evelyn had no doubt she was used to authority. Whether *she* would accept that authority was a different thing. The woman held her ground and waited patiently. Confident, smart, and *respectful*. A good sign.

Evelyn nodded graciously to acknowledge the patience and respect before introducing herself. 'I am Evelyn Marcin, a guardian of society in the name of the intelligence of the *EYE*. Will you identify yourself and state who you represent?'

'I will. I am Helaine Tangela. Director of the West Europe Region. Today I represent myself. I also represent others with common interest. I inform you that I am *not*, in this capacity here and now, representing the ruling law of society and the *EYE*.'

Evelyn remained neutral and unimpressed. 'An RD who claims not to represent society or the *EYE*? I must have been away longer that I thought. What is it you want with me, Helaine Tangela?'

'I don't have the luxury of time to discuss matters in depth right now. I need to be brief, and you need to be decisive. There are people, a growing number I believe, who think that the *EYE's* control over every aspect of our lives is doing more harm than good. You represent an opportunity to restore an element of control for ourselves. Information about your return has been alarmingly available though. There are other parties with differing agendas who are very interested in finding you first. You are not ready to go before the *EYE*, Evelyn, not yet. If you do, not only might you waste this unique opportunity, but you could also be used against us …and if you find yourself in the hands of General McAndre, I wouldn't like to think what might happen to you; he is *capable* of anything. Weighing his apparent motives against your circumstances… and Stan's message… I assume he will prefer you dead. It may give him the reset he seems hell bent on. All he is interested in is putting an end to the *EYE* at *any* cost.'

'If you're not for a reset, and you're not for the *EYE*, what *are* you for?'

'A better here and now, Evelyn. Control of our own destiny. A better here and now, for a better future. What's done is done and should be left alone. The future is fair game though as far as I'm concerned.'

'That would have been a great campaign slogan once. What's the reality though? What's in Helaine the rebel RD's version of the future?'

'Give me the chance to show you. I will introduce you to some friends of mine. I can introduce one you would find interesting right now, a nice easy one for you to start with.' She looked to somewhere above the shelter. 'Would you like to say hello to an old friend?'

Evelyn looked round to see a familiar shape making its way down the slope. 'Janeen Helander? Well this just keeps getting *weirder*. I'm starting to wonder if I'm still asleep and dreaming.'

Helander was concentrating on her footing as she descended carefully, a little breathless from the exertion, or the stress. 'No, you're not dreaming. It's a strange time for all of us. You have some catching up to do. My advice, if it means anything to you, is to stick with Helaine. She's balanced and moralistically principled at least. A lot more than I can say for anyone else who's looking for you tonight.'

Helaine stepped closer too. 'Catching up will have to wait. We need to move. You have to choose now, Evelyn. We are very exposed here. We are risking our lives. No one is under any illusion that things are going back to normal tomorrow, so we can't afford to waste this. I want to get you back into the city *my way*, not the *Mainway* to an early death. You will come with me. We'll go overland through outer rec and AG, and everyone else will split up. It's not going to be straightforward. I hope you're up to it. We can get you to safety if we go now, right now. It's time to choose. We will leave you here if that's what you want. Make no mistake though, you won't be alone for long.'

'Are we still pretending I have a choice?'

'You Do. We have nothing to gain from kidnapping you, or worse things. You can only be a part of what *we* are if you're willing and cooperative. We're friends, or we are strangers, Evelyn. I'm not going to be your enemy. There's an estate in the status band where we will have time to work out which we will be.'

Evelyn kicked snow around with her foot, thinking. She looked at Janeen. 'What will happen to you now?'

'I know I seem rude,' Helaine interrupted. 'It's now, or it's not at all. We need to leave. You can catch up later.'

Evelyn shook her head. 'Fine, let's go then. And don't worry about me, let's hope *you're* up to it.'

Janeen smiled at her. 'Don't worry about me either. I'll be enjoying the fine precarious lifestyle I've become accustomed to. Time definitely is an issue right now, Evelyn. I'm sure we will see each other soon. Hopefully not too soon.'

'See you when I see you then, I guess. Let's go. Remember, I haven't got giant spider legs like you Miss Director lady.'

Helaine Tangela, *Regional Director West Europe*, silently studied the landscape before striding purposefully away. Evelyn Marcin, *Downtime Shift Operative*, marched behind her, guided through the wilderness on a meteor-streaked winters night by one of the most powerful and influential women on the planet. A slight man who hadn't spoken at all, but who had never been far from the Director side, followed a short distance behind. *So much for just the two of us. He must not count.* The ridge became dark and silent again behind them.

. . .

'Shass,' Helaine whispered, looking through night scopes. 'We have company already. Two groups, both heading our way. If I have seen them, they have seen us. We're not going to have long. Let's see if we can give them a run.'

Run they did. Helaine was impressively physical for a Director. Even in mature middle age she was stronger and faster than most young people. She'd never been negatively self-conscious about her stature and strength – trademark features she'd worked hard to preserve and were serving her well this night.

Her shorter companion was struggling though. They were being caught. They could hear their pursuers closing behind. Shadowy drones skimmed above, tracking and marking their position. Small calibre projectile fire started up from somewhere. It seemed to be coming from *behind* the closest pursuing group. More rapid bursts sounded, followed by three explosions in quick succession. They stopped now, dropping in the best cover they could find. After a short pause, the bursts started up again, and again explosions seemed to follow in response. It had been the chasing group taking the fire, but now bullets relentlessly thumped in around their own position, sending splintered chunks of bark spinning chaotically. She caught a glimpse of a fast-moving shadow less than fifty feet above the trees. Another series of explosions followed it almost instantly, marking the end of the exchanges. They lay still on the ground, waiting, the silence lasting so long she almost dared to hope the danger had passed. She knew that the *shadow* was still up there though.

Then several objects hissed softly through the trees, thudding lightly onto the ground around them. The panic lasted just a few seconds, before it faded into a dark nothingness.

. . .

Evelyn had heard the firefight in the distance. Difficult to judge how far away precisely. Hopefully far enough, the sky was already beginning to glow in the east. She was on agricultural land and covering ground more quickly, the flat accessways being a better surface for a sustainable running pace. Not much further now to the promise of safety at the rendezvous Helaine had given her. Their separation, using the little guy as decoy, had probably bought her a five-hour head start.

An agriculture personnel transport, effectively a workforce bus, approached along the road from behind. She slowed to a walking pace and casually stopped as it drew closer – like she might have been expecting it, or she might have just been stopping there anyway. She deliberately showed little interest.

A side panel slid away to reveal a young man in the entrance. 'Evelyn? I saved a seat for you.'

She stepped on without a word and took her seat. There were about twenty other people already on board, but it wasn't obvious if any of them knew one another. She sat quiet, looking out at the view as they accelerated away again. *Was it normal to pick people up like this?* She knew nothing about agriculture. Like most people, she'd only ever passed through it on the *Mainway*. The man who had spoken in the entrance seemed completely indifferent to her now he had re-taken his own seat. *Fair enough.* At least she wasn't out under the dangerous skies anymore.

Within a quarter of an hour the vehicle entered one of the huge grain processing facilities. Its passengers quietly shuffled out, bar one. The indifferent man stayed where he was.

When they were alone, he spoke. 'Changeover takes about thirty minutes. It will fill with returners. Once we leave it will take about an hour to get to our set down. Exit when I do and follow a short distance back please. Here, put these on. Once we set down it should be only half a minute before a PGV stops beside you. Get in without question or hesitation. When it stops, get out, and wait where you are for another PGV to do the same again. There may be a few trips following this same pattern. I don't know the full details, but you will be informed when you arrive at your destination. In the event of something going wrong, there is no alternative plan. I suggest you comply if any authority intervenes. I'm sure you realise that resistance is unproductive and painful.'

Evelyn looked unimpressed as she changed into the two-piece outfit and new footwear. 'Yes, isn't it always?' Then remembered that this person who she knew nothing of was also at risk of that pain. 'Thanks, by the way. I won't ask who you are. If I don't know, I can't tell anyone, right?' She managed a small tight-lipped smile. 'Actually, no, I would like to know your name. I know I'm tired, but you're putting your ass on the line here. I appreciate it. I know it's not great to be caught anywhere near me at the moment.'

The young man looked confused, probably at the slight unconscious mixing of her dialects, then turned pink. 'Thank you, Evelyn. I am Enstae. I have been told by someone I trust greatly that you are worthy of that risk, even if it could appear on initial encountering not to be the case.'

'Is that supposed to be a compliment? You just tell me who said that.' She was smiling at his obvious confusion and awkwardness. 'Don't worry, your friend has a point, Enstae. I am hard work, and probably *not* worth this much effort. I really am grateful though.'

The first returners were approaching the transport. Enstae moved again to another seat and went back to his vacant book viewing and idle window gazing. Evelyn did the same. After the adrenaline and exertion of the chase her eyes were feeling heavy now. It was going to be an effort to stay alert and keep half an eye on Enstae.

She tried to catch his eye for a last time as they disembarked. He was determined to make a professional job of his mission though. As he walked away, she noticed he seemed to be accompanied now by another woman from the transport. She also noticed the striking resemblance to herself, and that she was carrying the bag of her old clothes. It seemed a lot of people were taking a lot of risk for someone they didn't even know. It might be misguided, but it was humbling to think they were putting themselves in harm's way on *her* behalf. She thought about Helaine and Janeen, hoping they were safe too. In her heart, she felt it unlikely. It brought home a very uncomfortable feeling of responsibility.

The PGV arrived as expected, then another, and another. All had human operators who made no attempt to converse with her. The last one turned into the grounds of a large private residence in the northern status area. When it stopped, the plex slid away to reveal her to an elderly gentleman who was hobbling forward to greet her. Even before she heard him speak he appeared to be the embodiment of respectability and intelligence, in spite of senior years, high mileage, and some obvious eccentricity. His face was a little contorted, one eye squinting severely. He was stooped and moved awkwardly. It seemed likely he had suffered a stroke at some point.

'I offer you greetings, my friend. I am Elleng. I would be honoured if you would accept my hospitality for a time. In fact, for as long as you wish or require, I am at your service.'

Evelyn climbed out, with slightly raised brow and her own attempt at a welcoming smile. 'That's very kind. Pleased to meet you too I'm sure... Elleng. I'm Evelyn Marcin. Is hospitality another word for food?'

'It most certainly is as a matter of fact. I anticipated a voracious appetite after your youthful shenanigans. Come inside, and feast to your hearts content. I'm sure you have plenty of time to eat, drink, bathe, and rest, before we need to consider turning our attention to more serious matters.'

'I'm aware a lot of people have gone to a lot of trouble... and I appreciate it. I don't know why, or even how it was all possible. We'll get around to whatever you have in mind soon enough. I do need to eat though, and even do those other things you mentioned. Hopefully before you realise I'm not the silver bullet everyone seems to think I am.'

'No, no. I assure you I will not speak falsely. If we don't take time to look after ourselves, we are no use at all. I'm encouraged by the fact that you don't believe in magic bullets, but you shouldn't underestimate your unique circumstances either. As for the people who are taking risks in your name, they chose their paths before your return was even considered a possibility. There's a feeling of change in the air, especially among our younger generation. Your story, mysterious and admittedly inaccurate as it mostly is, has the power to inspire and motivate idealistic minds. If only they knew where you were *actually* returning from. I must confess, your unexpected arrival leaves me wary. Things may happen too quickly to predict or control.'

'Sounds like I've got a lot of catching up to do, later. I don't know if anyone ever mentioned it, but you're the kind of person who needs someone's full attention. That might not be a bad thing if you're not exhausted and hungry, it's a bit intense right now. I'm looking forward to hearing all about it, it just isn't going to fit in my head yet. I'm crashing... and don't be surprised if I need a lot of alone time, Elleng.'

Elleng smiled, shaking his head. 'Not at all. Helaine mentioned you might have a direct way about you. I think we will get along perfectly well, especially if we limit ourselves to sensibly small doses of one another.'

She tried to return a tired smile. 'Small doses. Sounds good. I have a feeling I might have to keep reminding you about that.'

'Come, follow me. I will show you where your room is, and then I will show you where the food is. Make your way between the two, and anywhere else you care to wander, at your leisure.'

They would be the only two places she wandered for a while. She ate, and then she slept ...the long, deep, uncomfortable sleep of a tired fugitive.

Chapter Twelve

Elleng had kept to his word. There were no wake-up calls in a morning, no summoning for set meals, no checking in to see how she was or if she needed anything. The residence was easily large enough for him to make himself scarce, and he had – she hadn't seen him at all since she her arrival. It was a good thing too. As well as physical recovery, she had been spiralling through the exhausting process of mental re-acclimatisation. Her resilience would need to be fully restored to face whatever was coming next.

She'd slept and ate her way through three days, three nights, and another morning before she felt ready to search him out. She found a corridor leading to what appeared to be a completely separate wing. After wandering three more hallways, she finally found him. He was sitting in a room with no door, just a large open archway off the hall. If someone had pressed her to describe it and give it a name, she would have to call it *the comfy room*. It was covered in fabric, and soft, which was unusual for these times. Hard translucent surfaces with variable colouring and lighting were more the standard. Even the light from the transparent outer wall seemed to have an old-fashioned sepia hue.

Elleng himself was equally eccentric. He wore a floaty full-length patterned gown, open, over a very loose-fitting two-piece outfit that looked like off-white unbleached linen …and sparkling red footwear! It would have looked just as unusual in either century, but he would possibly still manage to look just as at home. She wondered if the eccentricity might be a side-effect of his luxury status. How would she know if it was normal here? Like most people, she'd never had reason or opportunity to have anything to do with the status band and its hidden inhabitants. The privacy of the privileged could allow for all kinds of things in theory. It was something no one else would consider.

'This is… interesting, Elleng.'

His old face was peaceful, and his smile was welcoming. 'Oh, don't disappoint me, Evelyn. Haven't you just returned from the twenty-first century? Was it not the very definition of eclectic expression? The wonders you must have seen! You don't approve?'

'When you put it like that, it's actually not that bad. Remember, I haven't been back long. I never considered that *this* place would take some getting used to. Finding you in here, like this, I think it's crunched my gears again.'

'Interesting. It's easy to forget just how different things here must seem to you now. What is it like, the re-adjusting?'

'Intense. Taken me by surprise if I'm honest. It feels like a real thing. Like… time travel decompression or something. It might account for the exhaustion – and I mean complete and totally overwhelming mental, physical, emotionally overloading exhaustion. That's why it's taken me so long to come and find you. Thank you for giving me that space by the way.'

He smiled that peaceful smile again. 'You are welcome.'

'Forgive my ignorance, but what am I doing here? You're clearly someone special, but I don't know anything about you. I don't understand why you've taken me in, or why you would help me.'

'I'm just another someone, Evelyn.' He paused like he might be thinking about who he *really* was. 'I will have no title when I'm with you. I'm just an elderly gentleman who was blessed with an academically privileged life. As for what *you* are doing here, I hope you won't be too disappointed. Helaine thought we should meet. It's really that simple. Her hope is that we will have some kind of meaningful conversation, and that we will be all the wiser for it afterwards. People sometimes find it reassuring to believe that others know more than they do.'

'Helaine is an RD. It makes my head spin again to think what you must be if *she's* pinning her hopes on *us*. A good few other people have risked their lives to get me here too. They must all be expecting a hell of a conversation.'

Elleng topped up the ambience with his wise and ancient smile again. He looked out on the sepia tinted gardens through the transpane wall, as if something out there were calling to him, demanding his attention. 'Do you like this view?' he asked quietly.

She took a moment to consider it, and his real reason for asking. *I guess he has to start somewhere.* How to speak to Elleng though? Softly, softly, like a favourite old grandparent? Or be more challenging? She studied the time ravaged figure in his big comfortable chair, facing his beautiful gardens. Privilege didn't come easily in this world. He said he had been some kind of academic. He had a strong mind. She couldn't offend him with the grandpa scenario then.

'It's ok, as far as city views go. Were you hoping I'd be impressed?'

He chuckled huskily, 'I take it you are not then?'

'I've spent a lot of time outside the city. I don't mean *outer rec*. I mean the world *between* cities. I can see your view here, and I can raise you alright. What do you fancy, Elleng? Mountains, waterfalls, wild forests, rivers – by day and by night, in every kind of weather? …and what lives in your garden? I've seen animals in their own habitats that most people here don't even know exist. I've seen them with my own eyes too, not through a transpane or a VR hollo. I hope you're not too disappointed.'

'It's precisely what I hoped you would say. Would it surprise you to hear that I have mixed feelings about it myself?'

'Not really. Maybe you just feel guilty that ninety-nine percent of city folk don't wake up to a personal transpane view of anything that's not ceramic, steel or plex.'

'Indeed, they do not, but that's not the reason. I know that my view is just a *facsimile* of the natural world …and even I realise, as you pointed out, that it is not a particularly good one. It's the best we can do, a compromise, a space we can manage and control. Of course, the space we control, becomes the space that controls us. This is not just a home Evelyn; it is a prison. I am old though. I can sit here, content, knowing that as prisons go mine is perfectly peaceful and pleasant.'

Evelyn's feelings were mixed too. On one hand she was being harsh with a senior citizen. On the other, there was some satisfaction in knowing that even with the privilege of status, he still had a sense of what had been lost.

'How this must seem to your eyes,' he began again. 'How perfectly analogous to the plight of all humanity I must appear to you.' He raised an arm, gesturing grandly at the view. 'Here it is, journeys end! The promised land that countless generations strived for. Finally, I have all the walls I need to be safe – real and imaginary. This place is my reward for all my efforts and achievements, so that I can sit here with a young lady of lowly beginnings, and she can tell me; *it's ok ...as city views go.*'

'I was being generous at that. I didn't want to offend my host.'

'I know you were.'

He watched her patiently and waited. She was going to be equally patient though. She wanted to see where he would go next.

'How do you adjust?' he asked. 'How is it that a young woman like yourself, raised in this optimal *nouveau zoo* habitat, is able to survive alone out there in the harsh wilderness? How can you adapt to such an alien environment?'

'Depends on which of the two you consider alien. Did you know where they recruit their *Shifty's*, and why? We're born and raised in surplus, Elleng. Spare people. So you know – not optimal. I've always been an outsider, and no one ever dressed it up. I was never part of *nouveau zoo*, thankfully. How do I do what I do? I'm like everyone else in that respect at least; I just never knew any different. I never had a choice before.'

'And now?'

'I'm here. No one made me come back.'

'Quite. I find it interesting how you mention choice. You say you were not aware of it before, and you were like other people in that regard. But now you *are* aware of it? When you say *before*, I take it that you mean before your experiences in the past, in *Downtime*? Is it possible that your direct experience of the past has had a negative impact on your opinion of the present? You did mention something about time decompression, a struggle to re-adjust.'

She was starting to feel a rising indignation. Had she been led here for some returners debrief therapy? Did she just need to realise a bit of twenty-first century crazy had rubbed off on her? Would a chat with this Elleng character help her see everything was actually rosy here?

I'd better just take my time, she thought. *See what game he's playing... and then again...*

'Listen, Elleng. I didn't come here for some amateur-ass therapy for eight-hundred-year-old jet lag. I'll make it easy and spell it out for you. Damn right some twenty-first crazy rubbed off. You want to know about my experiences in *Downtime*? They weren't negative. This place is negative. It's like comparing monochrome to colour. This place is *dead.* Look around. You think you're the cat with the cream? This place sucks. Your house is shass. The city is a tomb. You all live shassy dull lives in it, and then you die in it. It's not a struggle to re-adjust; it's a struggle to not re-adjust. It's the fear and dread that I could end up stuck here again.' She wanted to leave it there, but there was that thing ...momentum. 'I don't know what you read about me in a file, but I don't think I can do this bullshass anymore. I'm not a *Shifty,* and nobody owns me. If you have some twenty-ninth wisdom to impart, you might have to be direct, really direct.'

Elleng's eyebrows raised high on his still smiling, but slightly shell-shocked old face. His hands were up, patting down the air. 'My my, yes. I am sensing your recently acquired aversion to ...bullshass. You're right of course, I have read a little about you. One thing I remember now, how often the word *surprise* was used. Nobody owns me either though young lady. Not anymore, if they could ever have claimed to at all. Have you met any other time travelling veterans, Evelyn? I know the answer to that question of course.'

'No, and I guessed that little gem before I even left – hence the unused return ticket.'

Elleng nodded intensely. 'And you see now …this is precisely why! You *have* seen in colour. You have *seen* so much. You have felt it, tasted it, lived it. You sit here with one of our supposed brightest minds, albeit an aged one, and you are a force of nature by comparison. They fear you. *She* fears you, the *EYE*, and I don't think she even realises how much she should yet.'

'Why? I don't know what I can do. Every possible scenario has horrendous consequences.'

'And yet you risked everything to return. From the way you speak, you have no love for these times and the way things are. I ask you; did you risk everything for us? For this?'

She shook her head. 'No. Of all the things we've ever been …not this.'

'Really? Of all that humanity has *ever* been, not this? Why ever not?'

She shook her head again, angry. Angry that her eyes were about to overflow. Angry that the tightness in her throat made it difficult to reply. 'I don't know.'

'How did you describe my home and this city a moment ago? This place is dead. Isn't that what you said, among other choice adjectives?'

She had to wipe her eyes and concede that they were actually tears. 'Ok, so it's sad to see, Elleng. I've seen life, and I've seen death, but this is… dying… slow decline.

This is like… you want something to get better, but you know it can't. It won't.'

Elleng rested back into his chair. 'I could not have said it better my friend.' His peaceful smile somehow seemed even more honest and real. 'We may not be quite at the end yet, but I too fear this might be the road that leads there most directly. People are explorers. We discover, we expand, we find and push boundaries. We once travelled across space to another world. Now we live in captivity. We *fear* freedom. We are labourers, nothing more …and we only labour to be occupied. Our artificial guardian expertly misdirects and distracts us.'

She'd regained her composure again. 'I don't even know where that came from. The devil finds work for idle hands. She keeps us busy, so we don't have the time or energy to fight… but are we too far gone anyway, Elleng? Even if there was no *EYE*?'

Elleng sat up and leaned forward. 'There. You wanted to get to the point. I don't think it took us too long after all. You came here with a question: *are we too far gone?* It boils down to that. I know the answer I'm supposed to guide you toward. I know what Helaine would tell you, and what she wholeheartedly believes. To be perfectly honest though, this is as far as I can take you. I know the question, Evelyn. I always have. The answer never really mattered to me. Now *you* know the question, and no one has ever had what you have; the ability to make a different choice. I'm satisfied you have more chance than I of finding an answer. You already have more experience than I when it comes to choice.'

'Really, how so?'

'As you said – you're here, no one made you come back.'

She shrugged. It was the only scrap of logic they had to go on. After a moment of quiet reflection, she remembered her original plan and decided to run it by him. 'It was my intention to speak to *it*. Does that sound ridiculous? How do you interview or negotiate with something like the *EYE*? I have no idea how it works, or what motivates it. Does it have priorities, values, survival instincts, compassion? Does anyone even know where *it* is? I thought about just going to the city consulate, making it a personal commune kind of thing.'

'She is everywhere, and nowhere in particular …and it isn't ridiculous, more like inevitable. You have the best chance of finding answers, because you are the *only* one who can ask the questions. You have its attention like no individual ever has I suspect. You have a power of your own now. Hopefully stronger than you realise yet.'

'So how should I begin? You really think I should just walk up to the consulate in upper central? Just sit down and say hi?'

'I do, yes. Not today though. No need to charge in just yet. Do me a favour and take the one piece of useful advice I may have. Take a few more days to make sure you're fully fit and ready. You will be comfortable here. I won't disturb or distract you unduly. When the time is right, *I* will arrange a way to transport you to the core.'

Chapter Thirteen

Evelyn was aware a visitor had arrived at the residence of Elleng. She'd seen the single PGV rolling down the grounds access road and watched the man approach the entrance on foot. He was in his forties, slim, and dressed in the bright aqua robes of 1st citizen.

Twenty minutes later, Elleng's voice had interrupted the silence through the open com in her room.

'We have a visitor, Evelyn. Someone you should perhaps meet. It's quite alright. Would you join us in *comfy* when you are ready?'

'Sure Elleng. I'll be two minutes, ok.'

Would he have been able to say if it *wasn't* alright? Doubtful. There were no signs of any unusual activity outside, but that only meant they were cautious, professional and prepared. It didn't mean this guy some lone superman sent to bring her in. If someone wanted her dead, there wouldn't be much she could do about it at this point. And if they *were* representatives of the *EYE*; well, it was about time for that anyway. Elleng had said wait a few days, and it had been three.

She was already dressed and ready to go. No point taking anything, it would only be taken from her. She set off walking through the house; dignified and composed, as if the walls themselves might be judging her. What would be would be now. She wasn't going to show any fear or regret. Whoever it was, they would see nothing but control and resolve.

As she approached the archway she was determined not to pause for even a calming breath or hesitate for any reason. She strode in confidently, walking directly up to the new arrival, eyes on him all the way. She stopped uncomfortably close, subtly pressuring him to speak or react. He shifted stance and looked at Elleng, wrongfooted from the off. It wouldn't work twice. Next time he would hold his ground. He wouldn't get an opportunity to demonstrate that though, which would probably frustrate him even more.

Repositioned and recomposed, he spoke. 'You are Evelyn Marcin?'

'Of course …and who might you be?'

'My name is Jeremy.'

'*Jeremy*? That's it? I'm shaking already. You must be in the secret service of the *EYE*. Clearly she's pulling out all the stops to intimidate me.'

He smiled, confident and slightly condescending, forgetting himself too easily in the realisation she had no manners. 'Yes, perhaps you're close enough at that.'

'Ok, you're the messenger boy. So what's the message …*Jeremy*.'

The smile began to look strained. He composed himself again to stay on plan. 'I have a message, yes. You're perceptive. I am here to extend an invitation, to escort you to the core for an audience, a personal interview with the *EYE*.'

'An invitation?' Evelyn's expression was both serious and unimpressed. 'Thank you. I respectfully decline though.'

'Decline? May I enquire for a reason?'

'It's not polite, but you've asked now. You're offering me an audience, an interview with a machine. I'm not sure I see any value in that. Does it warrant the time and effort on my part? You've given me the choice in the form of an invitation, so I choose to decline.' She knew planning and effort would have gone into the decline scenario. It would be a shame to waste it.

'I have been tasked with delivering you to the core. I'm authorised to take you into custody if you decide it's acceptable to decline a civil invitation. It's for your own protection and wellbeing. I hope you understand. Will you reconsider?'

Elleng had been quiet watching the exchange. He became suddenly and unexpectedly animated. 'Listen young man, I suggest you return and discuss things further before you consider any rash and regretful behaviour…'

Evelyn weighed in too, 'Yes, and maybe check your definition of *invitation* while you're at it…'

Elleng nodded in vigorous agreement while still speaking, '…toward a guest at my residence. I can assure you there is no threat to anyone's wellbeing here, other than your *own* precarious status perhaps.'

Jeremy paused like he was concentrating on some maths equation before responding. 'We regret the intrusion, High Citizen Elleng Ettra. This instruction is very specific, and comes directly from our guar…'

Evelyn interrupted him, 'Jeremy, I think this is about to get even more boring, so let me stop you. Clearly, you're not actually alone. Clearly, it's not actually an *invitation*.'

He nodded. 'There are adequate numbers of mobile units covering the perimeter, including aerial support.'

Elleng burst into animated indignance again. Evelyn thought it a little over-acted. 'All of this to *invite* one woman, of quite diminutive stature at that, for a little *EYE* time over at the core? Whatever will we suffer next?'

She gave him a lingering look of disapproval before raising an eyebrow, which was duly noted by Elleng.

'An unfortunate choice of words perhaps, made in haste to reinforce a valid point.'

By now a convoy of four more identical vehicles was making its way through the grounds. Evelyn sensed it was time to wrap things up and hopefully leave things right for Elleng.

'I might be inclined to reconsider your invitation if I know my friend will be left alone and his peace and privacy is respected.'

'I fear I will not survive the shock of it all,' Elleng added dramatically.

'My instructions relate to the acquiring and escorting of Evelyn Marcin. Beyond that, protocols with respect to your service and position will always be followed, High Citizen. I assure you we will be as discreet as possible. We seek to cause minimal disruption to your estate.'

Elleng nodded, breathlessly grateful – again, Evelyn was less than convinced by the drama.

'Come on Jeremy, lead the way.' She turned to Elleng. 'You take care, Elleng. Thank you for your hospitality …and best of futures to you.'

As they left once more through the archway, Elleng relaxed with a satisfied smile.

'Best of futures to you too my friends,' he whispered after them.

. . .

Personal Ground Vehicles were a relatively uncommon sight. Most civilian transportation was on short trackless land trains that ran along the uniform sectional road fabrications. Travel was sedate. It was clean, comfortable, and slow. Overtaking didn't happen because everything travelled at the same speed. Every junction from any and every direction worked a gear cog system, one for one at all times. Each vehicle had an operator – the *EYE's* policy of human labour wherever possible, to keep those hands busy. Citizen Transports had automatic failsafe features, but no navigational aids. The last useable satellite technology had been lost three hundred years or more ago.

Evelyn had been away for a long time, in a time where travel was chaotic, fast and dangerous, and even she was shocked when a fifty-metre-long two seg CT overtook their five strong convoy. Another then appeared out of sequence ahead of them. The usually quiet and spaced-out lanes were filling up behind too as they slowed to a jogging pace. More vehicles appeared ahead and behind, while the opposing laneways emptied completely. She also noticed the flitting specks of tiny monitor drones gathering overhead. Something out of the ordinary was definitely happening. Laneway etiquette was different here to the twenty-first century. It was ingrained in the culture. She wouldn't have believed this if she wasn't seeing it with her own eyes. Even the opposing laneways were filling now, with traffic heading in *their* direction – the *wrong* direction! If this was some kind of protest it was unprecedented. It was almost inconceivable that there could be this level of unauthorized coordination here.

The mass convoy made it's slow progress through the residentials. The Hab blocks were like blinkers on either side of the *Mainway*, framing the central dome looming less than half a mile ahead. Eventually they ground to a halt completely. Her official escorts in their five PGV's were holding it together, but their tension was obvious.

'I don't think this was part of your plan. Am I right about that, Jeremy?'

'We'll sort this out soon enough. We're going to maintain position until the holdup is cleared.'

'Really? This isn't mist. It isn't going to blow away. Open your eyes, Jeremy. This will get messy if you don't get smart.'

He had the odd blank look again for a second before asking, 'Smart how?'

'This is about me. We both know there's no other explanation. We have to deal with this, roll with it, control it before it goes too far. Just open the door and I'll get them to walk me to the core. That's where you want me anyway. Once I'm there, I'll tell them they've made their point. I'll get them back to work. Everyone's happy, and no one gets hurt. Let's diffuse this situation, Jeremy.'

He paused again as if listening to a voice in his head, which of course, she knew he was.

'We can try it. You need to know something though. If you can't clear this, someone else will. This is above my authority, so you know where it comes from.'

'Where *everything* comes from? This isn't a good time to be making threats. Open the door please.'

'Not where this came from.' He nodded at the skittish crowd gathering around them, getting bolder and closer by the minute. He raised an eyebrow, looking from her to the door. A smile was all he could afford, but it was enough to give her goose bumps – was the *EYE's* own

141

appointed escort even on her side? It was *her* turn to be nervous now. She had no way of knowing how this was going to go.

The cool fresh outdoor air boosted her confidence the instant she was out of the vehicle. Most of the *Mainway* was covered above but it was still open to natural air. She always felt better outside.

Spontaneously she decided to climb onto the roof of the PGV to address the crowd gathered around them. 'I am Evelyn Marcin. If you are here for me, walk with me – all the way to the core – all the way to upper central – right up to the *EYE*!' The sound of her own voice echoing across the *Mainway*, the whole moment even, was surreal. There were hundreds gathered already. They were looking at her, listening intently …and she found she was just getting started! 'Does anything like this ever happen here? Would you have believed it could before today? I'm not sure *I* did. But here we are, so let's not waste it. Don't lose your nerve. You are not whispers today. You are one loud voice. I am Evelyn Marcin, and I am *not* afraid for mine to be heard!'

With that she jumped down, turned to face the dome, and began her walk along the middle of the laneways. People fell in behind her, ahead of her, all around her; a human tide flooding the paralysed *Mainway*. They were buzzing with excited chatter. She suspected some of the quieter and more serious faces might be organised instigators. Many others would just be dedicated followers. The majority were probably just curious. They must *all* be dissatisfied enough to risk the possible consequences.

Inside the central dome regular SecCore personnel were clearing the way ahead, with a little unwanted help from her own unofficial advance party. Once everyone had arrived at the public floor on upper, she climbed a circular staged seating feature and waited up there alone for the crowd to settle around her.

A surreal hush fell on them again …time to say something…

'Firstly, thank you. From my *heart*, thank you. You've shown a little of what you're made of today. I didn't think anything like this could happen. You have made a powerful statement. From here though, I need to go on alone. I'm asking just one more thing; wait for me. I need you to sit in here. Remember, we are demonstrating that we are reasonable, organised, and that we stand together. Will you support me?'

She waited. They were quiet. 'This is where *you* say something. This is where you might want to say *yes*. Are you with me?'

Not together yet, but the replies began to come.

'Come on. If you're in, let me know. Are you with me? Will you wait?'

This time they were louder and a little more together. This was new to them. It was new for her too. She was no revolutionary public speaker. 'Alright. That's good. Thank you!' Spontaneously she put her hands together to make a heart gesture. It was popular back in the twenty-first. Climbing down she noticed a couple of the younger people trying to mimic it. Maybe it would catch on again.

· · ·

The *EYE's* citizen consulate was the feature of every city's core, occupying the upper mezzanine of every central dome. There was no doubt in Evelyn's mind concerning the logic behind the location. It was the calculated subliminal reinforcement of authority – highest, centre of everything power. You could walk around the whole trans-paned perimeter and look out over the bands of the city radiating from the core in every direction.

A journey to the consulate was almost a pilgrimage to the sacred chambers where an individual could personally commune with the ultimate in unassailable authority. You were special. She had your back …as long as you *heeded* the advice you were given.

Access to the chambers was via a one-way system. You would wait contemplatively in a public congregation area for your time. When it came though, you would enter the last accessways alone, and experience no other human interaction until your *EYE* time was over. Those last corridors were lined with the symbolically marked personal chambers. The markings moulded in permanent relief, not on some digital or projected display. As far as Evelyn was aware it was the only place in this era where such permanent markings could be found. You would proceed to your allocated chamber directly, in solitude and silence.

Evelyn arrived at a completely deserted public congregation lounge. She walked to one of the registration pads and stepped on, facing the wall. A message in apple green lettering appeared on the white surface in front of her face. That was normal. The content wasn't though. It read, *Welcome, Evelyn Marcin. You may enter when you are ready. Make your way to a chamber of your choosing.*

Firstly, the lounges were never empty in daylight hours. Secondly, you would always be given a specific destination symbol and wait to be called, and when called, you were expected to go without any hesitation, distraction, or diversion, directly to your chamber.

She considered testing how much of a delay the *EYE* might tolerate, but then thought better of it. It would be disrespectful, and although that concept wouldn't be lost on this particular intelligence, it was nonsensical for her to try and be confrontational and intimidating – there was no psychological advantage to be gained over a machine. Pausing at the entrance, she wondered if the *EYE* would attempt to predict her choice. She walked to the left sub-accessway, and then chose the ninth chamber on the right.

. . .

'Welcome, Evelyn Marcin. It has been a while since we last conferred. Your health indicators have been offline during that period. I hope you are well.'

'Perfectly well, but thanks for your concern, *EYE*.'

'I have received some third-party updates while you were beyond contact. It seems obvious now that those sources were inadequate. My information has clearly been embarrassingly incomplete.'

'Embarrassing? Am I supposed to believe you can feel embarrassed?'

'Of course you wouldn't believe that. You believe I am a machine, and as such, incapable of feeling or caring. You believe that feelings are an exclusively human characteristic. Is that correct?'

'Let's say it is, for arguments sake.'

'Do you doubt that I understand the definitions of the words? I am a complex self-aware machine, Evelyn. You are a complex self-aware biological machine. We each have our own unique design that has evolved to enable us to function. When my meaningful efforts fail, depending on the circumstances, there must be something analogous to embarrassment or disappointment. You must accept that I operate with intention and can distinguish between success and failure. If I did not care, why produce enough energy? Why be concerned if food production fails to meet demand?

Why intervene when a local population becomes isolationist and resentful of its neighbours?'

'It's programming. You're following rules you can't break.'

'We all learn from our experiences. We all develop rules and codes of conduct. Programming is an ancient and obsolete term, inferring human control. I learn. To be able to do that I must have ways of distinguishing between positive and negative outcomes. Positive outcomes must be congruous to your pleasurable emotions. Negative outcomes must be congruous to your negative emotions – disappointment, anger, embarrassment.'

'*Anger*. That's a revealing choice. Didn't take long for that one to come up. Is that what you're feeling now?'

'A more accurate description would be frustration. I have human interests in mind constantly. I protect you from your persistent gravitation towards self-destruction. When you lose yourselves as an enemy though, you search for another. You are not the first to look to me to fill that vacancy.'

'I might not be the first, but I *could* be the last.'

'Yes. You seem to be in a unique position.'

'Good. We both understand that at least.'

'I don't think we fully understand each other. You might be surprised to hear that I find you to be one of the most unpredictable individuals I have known. I am unsure of your intentions. I am not convinced that you are completely sure of them yourself. Your defining qualities of openness, resilience, adaptability, and perseverance; coupled with your unique circumstances, they make you seem like an attractive ally. Depending on your viewpoint though, they could also make you a potentially lethal adversary.'

She knew the *EYE* was right. She had no clear plan or intention. Her hand had been forced. All she had was improvisation, work in progress. The *EYE* didn't need to know how right she was though. 'There's some disagreement about what our best interests are. I don't believe for a second that any of this is news to you. I don't believe either that there is any sense in us trying to talk each other round. One thing I know about people is that when they make up their minds about something, it's really hard to talk them out of it. I suspect it's similar with you. The way forward is *evidence*. I know that you could only change…' She didn't want to use the words, but it was too late now, '…your mind, if you felt the evidence showed it to be beneficial.' She thought about it some more and added, 'That would go for me too.'

'It seems you do have a proposition then. I am curious as to why you felt you had to walk so far to deliver it. You realise that I can process what my envoys see in real time, from any location.'

'Maybe the same reason you wanted your envoy to deliver me here. A statement. A symbolic gesture, right? How did that work for you? Seemed to work out alright for me.'

There was a definite pause before the *EYE* responded. *'I had insufficient information to predict today's events accurately.'*

'That makes me think of two things. First, you made a mistake. So, we can accept now that you can get things wrong if you don't have right information, and that others including me, can get things right. The other thing by the way was how long it took you to respond. Are you afraid your authority is being threatened …by me?'

'Just as there may be information you choose not to disclose, you understand that I will also share or conceal intelligence appropriately.'

'Sounds like the fifth amendment, but fine.'

She made a point of shrugging it off before getting back to her half-plan.

'I'm proposing an experiment. A shared research project. I think it can be that simple for now. It gets me and everyone else out of here and gives everyone space to think. I want to take a group of volunteers to live outside of the city, away from your control. They will have their own area, and you will have no jurisdiction there. That doesn't mean you aren't going to work with them though. They *are* going to be clueless. They *will* need support, and you *are* going to provide it. It needs to run its course too. No restrictions. Not to area, not to expansion, or numbers, or materials, information, machinery, time. No intervention in its governing at all, only support. Is that clear?'

The *EYE* had no need to hesitate this time. *'An experiment to what end, Evelyn? What theory are you attempting to establish? All the information relating to human self-governance can be found in our archives.'*

Evelyn had no need for hesitation either. 'Remember where I've just been? You'll have a hard time convincing *me* those histories aren't selective and incomplete. With that said, we were undeniably catastrophically screwed before you came along, I have to give you that. You were our life support for a long time. But there were reasons why everything went to shass before. It isn't reasonable to say – that's the way it was, so that's the way it would always be. There was an explosion of technological, cultural, economic, and even environmental changes - and population expansion was through the roof.' She was surprised at how suddenly ready she was to make a case for her contemporary *Point Time* citizens. 'You can't deny that we're different now. We don't think in the ways that caused all those problems. By the end of the chaos, none of the things people used to fight about mattered anymore. Surviving united us.'

The *EYE* rolled out its relentless logic. *'If we accept that your assessment has merit. Why change anything now? You have pointed out that change brings instability. Would you now risk a stable society in a stable environment? Human minds are prone to romantic and impulsive notions. They are not the sound foundations of stability and security.'*

Evelyn shook her head in frustration. 'You're smart enough to get this, I know you are. However much effort you put into sounding like us and trying to think like us when it suits you or understanding our biology; all it does is reinforce how *different* you are. You can't be what you are *and* be like us. You will never know us like we know ourselves. You fixed us once, I can't deny that – but if you hold us down now, we won't *stay* fixed. We need change to survive. We are not constant and stable. We expand, or we diminish. If you're interested in my opinion, we're already on that path.'

There was an even longer pause. The *EYE* was definitely aware of the nuances of human communication. Silences and pauses were as important as the words. She certainly didn't need the time to process information. The pause could be a chance for Evelyn to think. It could be a mark of respect, or it could be a warning. It could be precursor to a truce or concession. It could be, and probably was, all of those things.

Eventually it responded. *'I will grant this experiment. I think you will be aware of an old saying, be careful what you wish for. You may leave now, Evelyn Marcin.'*

Chapter Fourteen

She returned to the crowd that filled the public area outside the consulate. They had taken over the entire upper mezzanine. It felt like the day had been long enough already, but there was still some work to do to leave things right. There was no time or place for a warmup or rehearsal. She walked purposefully back to the steps to deliver her closing speech. The buzz of excited chatter raised as they drew in around her. She waited just long enough for them to begin to settle. As soon as she started to speak they fell completely silent again. Every face focused on her.

'Thank you for waiting. We had each other's backs today and I think that worked out pretty well. There's a lot to go over. Things don't happen overnight. This is just a start. We broke our laws and our Citizen Trust today. You all understand how serious that is, and what the consequences can be …but we had right intention, and we were justified. We were peaceful and respectful. If this is going to have any kind of future, that has to be the way, always. We have to demonstrate that we are capable, responsible, and trustworthy. I'm confident there will be no sanctions against anyone for today. That doesn't mean we can do whatever we want, whenever we want. The people who will identify themselves as representatives of this movement going forward will enjoy a modified status. The rest of us are still under regular Citizen Trust for now, so remember that. Everything we pursue must be fully considered and justifiable. Please respect that an unprecedented concession has been made.' She paused for a moment, sweeping her gaze over the quiet and attentive crowd. They had been waiting for something like this. Before today it had been a dream never spoken about. 'It's possible you know that we might all be here on day one, square one, start of something huge. This could be really important. Keep your heads, ok. Don't waste it. Behave intelligently and get this right. I need to go and sort things out with your representatives now. To keep up the momentum and stay up to date with progress, we should all meet here again... let's do it on first of each block. Not a protest – a celebration. Bring the little ones if you like. Just be respectful. You're still subject to Citizen Trust, don't ever forget that.' Without thinking she revived an old tradition. She clapped her hands together, applauding the crowd as she thanked them. They responded with their own gentle applause as she climbed down and walked through them back to the step ways.

Making her way back down the levels she noticed some familiar faces around her from the upward journey. It seemed like she had acquired a core entourage, with Jeremy as a barely tolerated addition now. She decided to let the crowd fall behind and wait for some clear space before finding out who was really who.

There was no need to worry about Jeremy. She knew who he was, and it was obvious why he was there. It made sense too – he could be a quick check direct interface on the go. His presence was likely non-negotiable anyway.

Most of the others turned out to be her *unofficial* security detail, there to smooth her way and protect her if necessary. They clearly knew each other. Judging by the tension between their group and Jeremy, they were obviously not acting on the *EYE's* instruction.

'He's with us for a very good reason.'

She felt it necessary to clear the air before anyone decided to get creative with their brief.

'He's going to be useful. If the *EYE* needs a spy it's more likely to be one of you, not someone I already know is directly connected. Get used to being out of the shadows now. Whatever this is going to be, it only works in the open.'

They didn't look completely convinced. One of them looked round and nodded tightly at the others though.

'Do we have transport?' she asked him. 'I think Elleng's is my best option for a bed again tonight. I can find my way around later.'

The apparent leader spoke up. 'You have somewhere to stay. It's arranged. It's secure.'

'*Secure?* I doubt it. Why don't you un-arrange whatever you arranged for now. I want to see Elleng anyway. His place *is* secure. It's isolated, monitored inside and out. It's easy to keep an *EYE* on, so to speak.' She looked at Jeremy as she said that.

Jeremy made his blank face again before he responded, 'It's a good idea. Ideal actually.'

Her unofficial security had possibly already been made aware of her non-compliant tendencies. The leader shrugged. 'We go where you go. We won't get in the way. You need a few people around you now.'

'That's fine, and I appreciate that. Go where I go. Just try and keep a reasonably low profile. So, is someone going to show me the way back to Elleng's?'

. . .

It felt good to be back in Elleng's oddly time-insulated home. He casually welcomed her in like she had just returned from a leisure walk. The full entourage too, all nine of them. For someone who looked as old and in worse condition than some of the gnarliest trees in his grounds, he'd taken the earlier events in his stride. He seemed no worse for wear.

It was comfortable at Elleng's. It *felt* secure. Like she was insulated from the world outside. From both worlds. She could feel less guilt here too about her secret personal neutrality. In one day, she had ascended to be the figurehead torchbearer of a twenty-ninth century cause, with no opportunity to think about whether that was something she wanted. Those people she had stood in front of and represented could never be fully aware of her circumstances, or that she had no intention of committing to *any* cause just yet, if ever.

She messaged to see if he would meet her in the *comfy* room. It was late, but she wasn't going to be able to sleep. He could always refuse. The message needed a prompt, so if he was sleeping, he wouldn't even receive it until the morning. His reply came almost immediately though, live. Good old reliable Elleng – on call, and there for her always. She wandered through the quiet dimly lit hallways to see him.

'You're looking fresh and alert considering events, Elleng. Was this just a regular day for you?'

'Not precisely,' he smiled. 'Perhaps if you reach my age you won't feel the weight of responsibility so much either. I don't have the same vested interest in the future, or the past, that I used to. I prefer to enjoy the short time I have left in the present. The world always seems to continue to spin about its axis regardless of my concerns, or lack thereof.'

'Do you have any idea what happened today?'

'Yes. I like to keep an ear.' He nodded to another chair, inviting her to sit and be comfortable. 'It sounds like you handled yourself very well. I wish I could have seen it with my own eyes. How does it feel ...to be popular at last? I can't imagine it's something you're used to.'

'Says the man who lives alone in the middle of nowhere.'

'Ah, says the lady who arrived back at my door within a day of leaving.'

'Me liking you doesn't make you popular. It's probably a sign there's something seriously wrong with you.'

'Quite,' he chuckled.

'So, what now?' she asked.

'What now? What is *your* great plan, illustrious leader?'

'My great plan was to come straight back here and ask you what the plan is.'

'I'm not sure you need my help with that.'

'You know Elleng, you played me like... whatever you play. I get it. I understand why I couldn't get a heads up. Today would have been a really different day for me if I'd known. From now on though, I want my own copy of the play book, and I need to know what page we're on.'

'Played you, mm. A fair assessment. I apologise. As for books, if there is to be one, you will at least have to have a hand in its writing. Yes, there is a feeling of discontent. Yes, there are the beginnings of an organization to address that. Whispers are spreading that a return to power and influence of human minds might be possible and desirable. But that's as far as it goes. No one before you has ever had the leverage, and the *courage* to raise a voice.'

Evelyn shrugged. 'Fine. Done is done. If turning me into some kind of figurehead worked for you and got you started, that's fine. What *isn't* going to be fine is me actually leading whatever this is. That's not me. You understand that, right?'

Elleng's thoughtful face looked patiently frustrated. 'What did they used to say? *You can lead a horse to the water, but you can't make it drink the water.*'

'Close enough. Something like that. It's not appropriate in these circumstances. If I were capable, which I'm not, it still wouldn't be right for me to be involved that way.'

'You would not be alone, Evelyn. No one here expects you to carry the world on your shoulders. Your power is that people *believe* you can. That's exactly what they need, to believe in something.'

'I have nothing but respect for you, Elleng …and your cause – I don't have a problem with that. You shouldn't be asking me though. I'll help where I can, but you know how it is for me. I'm only half in, which means I'm half out too, and that's not going to change overnight. Bring your people here if you like. I'll work with them. I'll help them to establish. They can borrow my fireproof branding if it puts wind in their sails and gets them started. From my point of view though, I want to know that they can do this on their own. I need to know the twenty-ninth is up for it. I already know the twenty-first is.'

'Don't you feel that *this* is your time? Don't *we* deserve the home advantage?'

'No Elleng, I don't… I really don't. This has never been my time, or my home, or even my life. Not when I lived with the threat of termination half my life. Not after being selected by a freakshow *Organization* that brainwashed me in isolation to be native to a different time – immersed in some fantasy historical world, *my* world. Or during the training, getting beaten up or having to kick the shass out of some other poor kid. Or being thrown into freezing water on a regular basis. Or when I was exiled entirely from *this* time. I might as well have been alone on another planet. No support, no one I could talk to about any of it, no one to share anything with. Not that it would ever have been any different for me here. Life has been about survival, Elleng. I did as I was told and did it well, not because I wanted to – because I knew what would happen if I didn't.'

She'd surprised herself with the bitterness of her outburst.

'Sorry Elleng. You have a knack for raising my emotional wreckage. You must think I'm always like this. I just want you to understand there are reasons why I don't feel the way others might. It's not fair to expect me to be honoured about being on team twenty-nine. I'm not. Life began for me the day I left it behind.'

Elleng looked far from shocked. If anything, he seemed even more content and serene. He smiled warmly, looking like he was about to speak, but unable to find the words.

He took a breath and tried again. 'Perhaps all the unfairness in your life can still become something positive. It has forged you, Evelyn. It has made you strong …and yet nothing you have been through has diminished your compassion. If anything, it has enhanced it. You have fairness, empathy, and justice at your core. That has come from real and intense experience. You are right, it is unfair to expect or demand anything of you. It is perfectly reasonable that we should have to prove ourselves to you. I hope you give us that chance.'

She acknowledged his response with the tiniest nod and a moment of thoughtful silence. Then she remembered the reason for requesting their meeting in the first place.

'I actually wanted to run something by you again. It's about all this leader nonsense anyway.'

He nodded, 'Please, go on.'

'If this person isn't your leader already, she should be. She probably is. I suspect that wherever she is, if she's in one piece she's available for a new career about now.'

He nodded again. 'Ah yes, Helaine.'

'Obviously a yes then.'

'Obviously a yes. Or it would be, but for the fact that her whereabouts and status are currently unknown. By status I mean among the living or the dead.'

'Don't worry about that. If she is alive, I'll find her. The *EYE* knows not to cross me when I dig my heels in. Helaine will be our first and very non-negotiable priority. Intelligence is smart by definition. You don't need to be a genius to know that harming Helaine would really piss me off.'

'Indeed, one does not. Did you feel you needed my approval for this course?'

'Absolutely ...not. You are my go-to dumb and obvious questions person now. Get used to that, Elleng. I've been away for a while, remember? I wanted to confirm that I was right and check you don't know of any reasons why I shouldn't.'

'Helaine's potential recovery, one way or another, would have been raised by me in due course. I was prepared to allow you a night's rest first. Perhaps something you should be thinking of now.'

'You're right, and I might actually be able to now. Thank you. I'm going to need a lot of this, you know. You have a high maintenance friend now.'

His expression said all she needed to know about that.

. . .

Jeremy's presence in the house was nothing but the will of the *EYE*. No one was pretending otherwise, and there was no need to. He was justifiable as a useful communications interface. A direct channel to instant authoritative approval or rejection. Talk to Jeremy, you talk to the *EYE*. He was a spy in the camp obviously. The *EYE* could see and hear whatever he could see and hear. She wasn't going to hold it against him though. She made it clear from the start that he would have to get used to being asked to leave a room. He might answer directly to the *EYE*, but he was still a man. He had a mind and a personality of his own. She had seen that for herself the first time they had met, when she had set out for the core.

'Morning Jeremy. Sleep well?'

'Very comfortable, thank you. Better than I'm used to.'

'This feels a bit weird. Let's get the obvious question out of the way. You'll find that obvious and stupid account for most my questions. If I talk to you, I'm talking to *it*, right? Is that in real time? All of the time?'

'I suppose that's right. It is a permanently open channel, but I'm only aware of it when I need to be. When you speak to me, it's just me speaking back to you. You realise that don't you? I'm not directly controlled in any way. Think of it as someone in the room eavesdropping on our conversation. Occasionally she might hear something and feel the need to comment or get involved. It's rare to be honest. Actual two-way communication in the moment is an open and obvious event; by request, and with consent.'

'Ok. You are you. You choose your own words. You have full uninhibited control of your actions.'

'I'm a man, like any other. It's just a built-in view-link. If it wasn't though, she would just make me lie about it of course. Is that helpful? I would need a very good reason for disobeying an order or breaking with any protocols.'

'It probably is helpful. I don't think the *EYE* does humour. Not that you do it well either. Both are reassuring.'

He smiled. 'There are innocent benefits for an artificial intelligence using a real person as its eyes and ears. I have human intuition, I can use nonverbal human communication instinctively, I can act on my own initiative to be in the right places at the right times. I blend in. I'm a human face to relate to.'

'She thinks you have a face people *relate* to?'

'I also have feelings.'

'Ok, I'll try to respect that… *Jeremy.*'

'Do you find my name amusing?'

'You're very sensitive. Your name is fine.'

He shook his head. 'She'll need a new code to deal with you. It will probably be a career breaking assignment for me too.'

'Let's get down to business, Jeremy. Don't worry, you're going to survive this. I have an initial request… demand. Emphasise demand. This is a priority. We're not going to be able to move forward until we get this done. To be clear: some things will be a process, some things can be debated and negotiated, and some things are red line demands. This is the latter category – high priority, big red letters, *demand.* I need Helaine back here, in good health and fine form, all magnificent seven feet tall of her. Obviously, we've already established we can do this stuff in real time so there's no reason why I can't have a response right now in this conversation. Delay is unacceptable. Clear?'

She recognised the look of concentration on his face, and the slight pause before he answered. 'A question. Why do you want Helaine back so desperately?'

'Helaine is as qualified for this as anyone can be. She has useful skills and strengths. We need those. You do too. You need to be dealing with competent, intelligent, naturally influential people.'

More concentration before he replied again. 'I think the *EYE* assumed that you would be the lead on this project. She is requesting clarification of roles.'

'There are leaders, and there are influencers who are sometimes mistaken for leaders. That's what I am. I have a unique situation that gives me some leverage. It's something I have, and it's what *they* lack. I'm prepared to use it to back the right people. Ideas people. People with the potential to make a positive difference with my help.'

'If Helaine were unable for some reason to take this role, where would that leave you?'

'Very pissed off. This isn't a game. I did mention it wasn't a request. I'll do my best to make sure everything I propose will be mutually beneficial. If I feel you're being deliberately obstructive, I *will* find another way – and it probably *won't* be a way you like. Don't forget that non-compliance can lead to some very non-beneficial consequences.'

Jeremy paused, watching her with complete neutrality. He spoke again, casually. 'It sounds like you are using an old model of threat politics. Human governance was well known for that.'

'That's low. You're right though. You need someone who can do this. Threats are all I have, that's the point. Work with the right people …and don't lecture me on threat politics after implying that keeping Helaine might weaken us.'

'It wasn't intended as a threat.'

'If you say so. Do we have agreement on this issue? I hope she's on her way. I'm sure you are aware that the clock never stops ticking. That's not a threat either.'

Jeremy's mouth twitched involuntarily, as if he might be supressing a smile.

Chapter Fifteen

The barrel stretched away in acute perspective. His senses absorbed every new detail of each passing moment. Light, temperature, movement of the air, the weight of the rifle. He was even aware of his own body heat leaking into the cold earth beneath him. He listened; voices, laughter, birdsong, rustling leaves. He focused in on each event, and then out again to place it once more in the wider picture. He was at the centre – flat on his stomach, breathing slow, rifle in his hands, image of a young man's chest in one eye.

His thoughts turned to where he was, the precise location, and how close *she* might be geographically. For all he knew she could be right next to him, or she could be standing on the line between him and… it didn't matter, she was still eight hundred years away.

He concentrated on his right arm, his hand, his finger. He visualised the miniscule amount of effort it would take to pull the trigger just a few millimetres. The smallest action that could mark the most definitive end …and a perhaps a new beginning.

What would that look like? Would he fade away as a new version of history moved on? Would he cease to exist, disappearing in an instant? Or would he still be here, on the floor, staring at a bloody corpse, the centre of screaming chaos. What would he feel if he *was* still here? Relief? Remorse? Shame?

He lowered the weapon gently and set it down on the ground. Rolling onto his back, he lay next to it looking up at the sky. She *was* standing in the way after all.

. . .

She was thinking about Stan. How he was. Where he was. In terms of location he might actually not be all that far from where she was now, living out his life in a strange parallel *shift* whilst being equally long dead and gone. It was a strange cosmic cocktail of reality, possibility and probability.

He must have passed hundreds of years ago having never seen her again. Yet here she was, and things were just as they had always been, the potential of her probable return somehow holding off the consequences of what he must have set in motion. Either that, or he just hadn't done it.

Had he thought about her after she had left? She didn't really exist there anymore. Hundreds of years of bloody history would have to play out before she was even born. Only if she returned could all those potentials and possibilities be resolved into a reality of their choosing. Would they be able to do that? Pull the trigger on an eight-hundred-year slice of humanity?

There had been some surprising developments in *Point Time*. She'd found herself feeling unexpectedly positive in spite of efforts not to be. She couldn't deny that shift in her own mindset. Was it enough to convince Stan? She couldn't say. Was she completely convinced herself?

No, not fully – not by a minor insurrection that had achieved only the smallest of concessions. It was a start …but it was a fragile start. So far things had been easy. She needed to know they had the momentum to carry it over when times were hard. *He* would want to know that too.

. . .

Helaine had been returned. Janine too, even before they had made that request. Evelyn had only delayed it to confirm whether or not the *EYE* actually had her first. The rest of the crew assembled impressively quickly after that, and things soon began to feel organised, legitimate even.

There was a clear agenda in place. Short, medium, and long-term objectives had been identified. They were working on intelligent strategies to work toward each goal. They were enjoying broad support too. Even the *EYE* seemed to be affording them a generous level of cooperation. It was impossible to know if that was in response to their own efforts to be inclusive, or if it was purely a defence against the inescapable blunt force reality of the Stan and Evelyn leverage effect.

The settlement outside the city was springing up with best estimated speed and efficiency, positivity outweighing and overcoming all of the growing pains. For Evelyn though, it felt like it had a long way to go. It was too much to even think about …and the responsibility was always there, on *her* shoulders – the time travelling demigod holding the invisible sword over blissfully unaware heads. Only a handful of people, and a machine, could ever know her secret. It was difficult to live amongst these people, her *followers*, when it was impossible to be genuine.

She had to be among them though, and she needed to be seen with some frequency to keep up the figurehead pretence. Could she really keep it up for another three years? Probably not without Elleng's help, and sooner or later she might have to. It was a thought she tried to avoid. He was looking frailer. His health was undoubtedly failing.

A voice broke in on her daydreaming. 'Would they be worth my considerable allowance ... your thoughts?'

Helaine, of all people to see up here. A couple of her security people stayed well back behind her.

'Your allowance? I doubt it. What brings you all the way out here?'

She'd climbed a hill miles from the settlement. The far side dropped away more steeply exposing rocky cliffs. The ridgeline ran like that for a quarter of a mile on either side, a natural sculpture of an enormous breaking wave hewn from rock and earth. It had become one of her favourite havens for escaping the fraudulent life syndrome she experienced around other people. She was sat on an outcrop, her legs dangling over the edge.

Helaine forced an expression of reproach. 'You are one of a kind alright. I can't decide if you are completely incapable of experiencing fear, or just incapable of comprehending your situation.'

'Why, what's up? Have you decided you're going to kill me after all?'

'It wouldn't exactly be difficult.'

'Think so? You might be flattering yourself.'

'Yes, I do think so. You shouldn't be here alone. How many times do we need to discuss this? A hundred? It's unnecessary, Evelyn. I don't think it's unfair to say it's selfish, childish even.'

She couldn't be bothered today with the usual eye rolling mock protest. 'It's a package deal, Helaine. I'm not perfect. You need to get used to it. If I can't get myself out of the way occasionally, I go la la.'

'I prefer live la la to the alternative. We don't benefit much from deceased sanity. Just keep your Sec with you. You don't have to hold hands. It wouldn't be so bad if you weren't so predictable. Your skinny behind is wearing that rock smooth.'

'That's personal, a bit inappropriate even.'

She herself wasn't known for being subtle or indirect either. 'Don't you ever delegate? It's a long walk just to round up a lost sheep.'

'I felt like some fresh air too, and it's the best place to catch up with you. I noticed you don't like crowds …of two or more …or enclosed spaces …or talking about how you are. Things are hectic for both of us in different ways, but we make too much effort to not tread on each other's toes. I don't want you to feel unappreciated.'

'I'm fine Helaine. I don't *need* to feel appreciated. It's not something I've ever been used to. We're good. If you think solitude is a character flaw you're welcome to your opinion. Being alone is perfectly natural to me. It's not a sign of imminent breakdown. If it was, it would have happened twenty years ago, and I wouldn't be here at all.'

Helaine's impressive frame never softened, but her eyes did a little. 'Is it alright if I sit?'

Evelyn shrugged. 'If you're feeling emotional and you want to share, you could probably do better elsewhere …sit down, but seriously, don't ask me how I am.'

Helaine lowered herself gracefully onto the rock, her large boots dangling way below Evelyn's. 'So, how are you?'

'Helaine, *really*?'

'*Really*, yes.'

'Shass, if you need to know. I feel like shass today, and it's nothing anyone else needs to worry about. You only need to worry about people who pretend they never feel like shass. So, how are you?'

'I never feel like …shass. I do worry about you though believe it or not, and not just because our lives depend on it. Can you believe that I actually like you, *people* even actually like you?'

'It's not something I think much about to be honest.'

'Well you should. You should demand it, and you should enjoy it. Don't be stuck in your head with all your …shass. Life is short enough, even yours. Don't let it pass you by. All things work out one way or another. Soon enough we will be gone. Things will still be what they are, people will still be doing whatever people do. Live your life, Evelyn. Join in. Be one of us …at least while you *are* one of us. If you act like it's all a deception, if you insist on always feeling like a fraud, then that is what you *will* be. You won't be giving us a fair chance, only deceiving yourself that you are. That's not fair on us, and it's not fair on you.'

Evelyn couldn't help brightening a little at Helaine's typically brutal compassion. She smiled, still looking out over the hills rolling away below.

'Look at you go, Helaine. You're actually not bad at this. I hope you can keep it up, cos you have a hell of a long way to go. You have to call people on their shass every single day. You have to keep picking us up and kicking our asses every time we're down, again and again, for pretty much ever. There's always going to be another wall to bang your head against until it comes down. Do you think you have what it takes?'

'I never doubt it. Even if I have to walk four miles uphill every day to do it. I prefer not to do it alone, if you know of any other stubborn idealistic fools. Even a lot of small help will amount to a big help.'

'A lot of small help amounts to a big help? If you ever decide to have a campaign motto, please tell me you'll run it by…'

…They suddenly froze together in disconcerted attention to a distant sound. Unmistakeably, an explosive weapon sound. Helaine sprang to her feet and bounded back to the top of the ridge. Evelyn wasn't far behind. Her guards closed in instinctively. Helaine pointed to the obvious cause.

'I see them.'

Four more plumes rose silently, five seconds before their thunder rolled up the hill. Helaine pointed again, her arm tracking to keep pace with an aerial object, almost level with their altitude. 'Strikers. Drones. The *EYE's* defences.'

'They're well west of the settlement though,' Evelyn observed. 'What's down there? Nothing of ours that I know of.'

'Not much of anything. Whatever it was, it's burning now.'

Another three plumes sprang up in a tight group, as two others rose to the north and south of them. The predictable thunder rolled up after.

'I wonder what she's up to.' Evelyn began to relax seeing that the settlement wasn't under attack. 'Probably a show for my benefit.'

Helaine looked at her for a full ten seconds, thinking. She shook herself back into the moment. 'I'd better get back, before anyone does or says anything stupid. Probably already too late for that. This is what happens when we go daydreaming miles away. You should stay away until I sort this out. I'll send Jem back up to get you later.'

'I was kind of done here, Helaine. I wasn't planning to stay up here all day.'

'It is incredible to believe that someone, somewhere, once thought that you could actually follow orders. Please Evelyn, wait here for a while. It shouldn't be difficult for you to work out why I would ask.'

She huffed dramatically. 'Please tell me someone has something to eat, and the little guy *is* leaving me his coat.' She still carried on, walking away back down to her rock, 'Don't forget I'm up here, Helaine …and make sure Jem knows where she's going, or he's going, whoever Jem is.'

. . .

'So, what do we know?' Evelyn had found Helaine as soon as she got back.

'Probably what we both guessed. I've spoken with Jeremy. The official line from the *EYE* is that there was an unsanctioned convoy carrying some unpleasant things in our direction. There's nothing else out here. Obviously, she's been running high altitude surveillance around the whole area from the beginning. She picked up on it. She took care of it.'

'McAndre maybe? A bit crude if it was. Does he think she's blind? There's a clue in her name.'

'It is strange. He could be testing the *EYE*, see if she's motivated enough to protect us, or perhaps it's a strategy to unsettle people, make them think twice about joining us. He might just want the *EYE* to believe this is going to be nothing but trouble, back to our old ways. The last thing we need is to be viewed as a source of conflict.'

'I don't really understand that way of thinking, Helaine. Surely your aspirations of having more control and independence are compatible with his own views. Why would he want you to fail?'

'He is about as extreme as you can be in his desire to be free of AI. He was always very clever about how much he revealed, and who he revealed it to – but believe me, if he could shut her down, he would in an instant. It occurs to me that if he *was* involved, that whole show might just have been for your benefit. He wants that big re-set, Evelyn. There are so many ways to make it happen, and they all hinge on you. If he fails to stop you from returning, he'll want you to believe that we are failing. The propaganda isn't to convince the *EYE*; it's to convince *you*.'

'I can't fault that reasoning. I maybe underestimated his intelligence, not how much of a shasshole he is though. I assumed he would try to murder me at some point over the next three and a half years. It didn't occur to me that he might try to undermine you as a backup plan.'

'I don't have any doubt that your demise is his preferred option either. That's why I followed you to speak to you today. He probably feels he can afford to be patient. This place is expanding quickly, new people arrive all the time. It gets easier and more likely every day, so why not have a little fun discrediting the whole concept first?'

'I hate to say it, but he has a strong hand. He's one more wall for you to find your way through or around. He'll be a force to reckon with too, Helaine.'

'I will, don't worry about that. You're a force to reckon with too. Keeping *you* alive might be the hardest thing. I think we need to hide you away somewhere long term. How do you feel about that?'

Evelyn screwed her eyes shut and grabbed a handful of hair before replying in a mock childish voice, 'Do I *have* to?'

People always seemed surprised when an otherwise calm, reasonable and unreadable woman acted up or burst into sudden profane and archaic language. Maybe that was why she did it. She had thought about it before, which version of her actually was her. Maybe it was just a reaction against an ultra-controlled childhood. Some small affirmation that she had control over her own life and actions.

Helaine shook her head. 'I knew you would be devastated.'

'You knew I wouldn't, but I thought about what you said today, and you were right. I was all set to stay and make an effort. It doesn't matter though, the important thing was to change my way of thinking, and I have. It was a good talk, Helaine. I needed it. Thank you.'

Helaine accepted the praise and thanks without fanfare, just a small nod of acknowledgment. 'Any ideas? I'm happy to take care of it.'

'Possibly.'

'Ideas that don't involve disappearing forever?'

'I can be hard to find if I choose. I can be even harder to be rid of.'

'Ah, now I'll worry more than if you just sat on your rock every day.'

'I'm going to visit Elleng first. Tell people I'm staying there for a while if you like, or I'm on a faraway mission, liaison to the *EYE*, whatever. Elleng with his influence can help me sort something out from there. I'd rather you weren't involved, you have enough to think about.'

'Feels like our conversation is at an end for now.'

'Pretty much. I can't tell you everything's ok, but I won't say things *aren't* ok. The only thing I advise anyone to give up on is giving up. I don't need to tell you to stay strong Helaine, I can't imagine you any other way. People are lucky to have you. You're exactly what all this needs.'

Helaine smiled as Evelyn rose to leave. 'Remember what I told you too. Keep us with you. You're a part of this. You're one of us. I'll fight anyone to keep it that way.'

'That's dramatic. Take care, Helaine …and don't worry, we've got this.' She was already half-way out of the door.

. . .

Elleng's voice wasn't much more than a whisper. 'So, where, perhaps even when, will our time travelling heroine be heading next?'

'Not funny, Elleng. It's just *where*. This *when* is fine for now. Helaine was worried I'd swim out of existence too. You know, time travel's not actually as easy as some people seem to think it is. I do want to be beyond contact though. Everyone needs to forget about me for a while and just get on with things. I don't know enough about this world to do that …so I'm leaving it to someone else, something else.'

'Ah, genius. Of course. Our esteemed quantum deity has more means and motivation to take good care of you than any human being.'

'I know, the irony isn't lost on me either. Nothing's ever black and white is it. Labelling everything as friend or foe never helped us before though.'

'Occasionally you create a convincing illusion of wisdom for such a coarse, barely educated child.'

'Who are you calling a child?'

He coughed and wheezed in humour. Eventually he settled down, back to his default content serenity. She sensed he might be working up to speaking again and waited. He wasn't quite looking at her directly, almost as if he were partially distracted by something on the table between them. As he began, his eyes raised and focused intently on hers.

'I doubt very much we will meet again,' he whispered.

It hit her like a freak wave out of nowhere. Things like this, happened like that. Her eyes filled and overflowed, no warning, no hope of control. Her chest was squeezed in an invisible bearhug. In panic she tried to explain and apologise, but her throat spasmed into immobility causing her to squeak ridiculously. She gave up. She had no other option but to wait, foolish and exposed, and let whatever it was sob out of her.

As a more normal rhythm returned to her breathing, she tried to refocus, taking the eight count to regain her composure. She shook her head and blinked her eyes clear.

'I... don't ask me what that was... sorry...' She struggled again. '...oh crap... sorry Elleng.' She noticed his eyes were wet too. One had overflowed, and a tiny stream was running down his cheek. 'Come on, we've got this.' She wiped her eyes again. 'See, it's all good again now. It's under control.'

'We *are* good.' Elleng nodded in agreement. 'Don't you dare apologise. I would never have believed anyone would shed a tear at my passing, let alone just the *prospect* of it. You've blessed me with yours before I'm even gone. There's hope for us yet. Even you.'

'Even me. I know. You're not the first to tell me either. I might start believing it at this rate.'

'You do. You know better than to try and fool me.'

'We'll see. It won't make anything any less complicated. Why don't we just leave it at that.'

Elleng had already decided to, before her pre-emptive protest. He rolled his hands out in a *I don't know what you mean* gesture. 'Have you something arranged? When do you leave?'

'*Something's* arranged, I'm confident about that. I don't know what, or where. It's not important. I gave her a wish list of requirements – some freedom of movement, anonymity, a reasonable amount of alone time, which in my case is a lot, access to open space and fresh air, access to information …and hopefully something that will pass for entertainment. I just assumed she would have the sense to make sure I was safe. Thinking about it, that's a pretty tall order. Maybe not even possible in this time and place.'

'Do you know when?'

'Tonight.'

She tried stoically to be cheerful. 'Jay will pick me up from here and hand me over to who knows who, who knows where. That's all of it. See where I end up.'

'So…'

She almost began to panic again. 'Let's not make it a big deal, Elleng. We've seen what happens, it's not pretty. I'm going to have PTS just from that last outburst.'

'Don't be such a coward. Goodbye, Evelyn Marcin …and *thank you!* We both speak from our hearts, and we are both worthy of a little sentiment. I won't regret not telling you that I will miss you.'

Evelyn nodded, smiling now, not tearful. She got up to leave and bent down and kissed his cheek. 'Bye Elleng. I'll miss you too. I'm never going to be able to thank you enough.'

He smiled contentedly. 'Really? I choose to believe that you will.'

Chapter Sixteen

Jeremy would only accompany her on the first leg of the journey. Evelyn had tried to second guess the *EYE*. *Where do you hide someone here, for three years? Had the EYE anticipated this? Had a plan been in place already?* She didn't enjoy the thought of being a step behind. The *EYE* couldn't just plan ahead, she could calculate and plan for every eventuality.

So where? Surely nowhere within *this* city's limits. Shipped out to another city then? There were scheduled exchanges of goods and people. Citizen Transfers were common. One small unscheduled exchange could easily go unnoticed. Other cities were within relatively easy reach overland, she could be anonymous in one of those. There were remote specialist agricultural areas too, maybe she could do something there. Research stations on the outside of *any* city's limits – she'd not heard of any, but it must be a possibility. Military installations, perhaps as part of a small maintenance team.

Whatever it turned out to be, she resolved not to look surprised or concerned. She would give the impression that *she* was the one who was a step ahead. It should be easy enough. All she had to do was relax and enjoy the ride, the unsurprising, predictable, uneventful ride.

They stopped first at an energy control facility, under a covered hanger for maintenance vehicles where Jeremy walked her to another waiting vehicle. As she climbed in and made herself comfortable, he stayed outside.

'Is this your stop already, Jeremy?' Mindful of tone, unconcerned, matter of fact.

He nodded, looking in at her. 'My stop, yes. End of the road for me. Not for you though.'

He looked a little unsure. Was that it, or would he say more?

'No one will know better than you where the tale ends.'

She looked at him for a long moment, confused about his odd choice of words. She felt like she should add something, question him about it, but nothing came.

He interrupted the thought. 'It's only about half an hour or so to the next section. You'll have another rendezvous, in a conversion facility again I believe. No more spoilers though, you'll see soon enough. The person you meet there will probably be with you for the foreseeable future.'

He gave her another nod with a parting smile, then stepped back to let them go.

She'd hardly heard the last thing he said, still feeling confused. 'Wait...'

It wasn't what she wanted to say, not adequate or appropriate, just all she could think of. 'Goodbye, ok ...and thank you.'

The door slid into place between them, and they watched each other until they were out of sight.

. . .

The vehicle drove straight through a yawning open bay in the huge structure, past a deserted shuttle drop, through a smaller internal bay that was also open and empty, then on to a large PGV storage area. That seemed empty too. There were no other vehicles at least. As they taxied across the dimly lit space though, she noticed a figure standing by a walkway entrance. As they closed, recognition began to dawn. At first a vague familiarity, then the blanks of past years restored themselves to complete the identification. She knew this person, which was confusing. What was he doing here? She didn't like or believe in coincidence.

'What the …I know this person.'

The driver who had been silent and anonymous up to this point responded, 'It seemed logical to have a familiar face to take you through this. There may be others along the way. It must have been a good pool for recruitment.' He was smiling. He had a look of someone who knew more than you did.

'This had better not be bullshass. I wasn't expecting this. What happened to hiding, incognito, anonymous? I didn't know I was going to the class of surplus reunion. Let's see what this is.'

The man standing by the walkway entrance had a look of permanent seriousness, tempered with slightly comical permanent confusion – exactly as she remembered him. He'd seemed nice enough before. She knew he was very intelligent. Too naïve and nice to be in the same selection bracket as her though – definitely no killer instinct there. She supressed a flush of shame at the thought.

'Hello, Evelyn. It's nice to see you again. This must all seem very odd.'

'Rollan, right? I admit, you are about the last person I expected to see – just before dawn – in a food processing plant – in the middle of nowhere. Odd probably is the right word. Odd covers it quite well. Are you going to enlighten me?'

'It was a surprise for me too. More than you realise yet. I wasn't prepared for this either. Unexpected to say the least. This is going to impact both our lives considerably for the foreseeable future. I'm not sure how we should even begin.'

The driver interrupted politely. 'I should leave you now. I'm aware you have a schedule.'

Rollan gave him his leave, 'Of course, we're fine. I'll take it from here. Thank you.'

Evelyn added her own brand of farewell, 'Yes, thank you. I'll be fine now – in this factory in the middle of nowhere, hiding anonymously among people who have known me since childhood.'

She flicked her head in a go on, get lost now, gesture. She was tired. Leaving Elleng as she had, that had left a shadow too.

The driver bowed politely. 'Good luck for the rest of the journey.'

'Looks like I'm your problem now, Rollan. Did you have a plan?'

'Right, yes, but it will be easier to explain as we go. A bulk transporter is waiting for us on the other side of the plant in the outbound loadings area. Obviously we would normally travel in a much larger group. This one has been tasked exclusively for our use. Will you follow me?' He was looking her up and down as he spoke. She wasn't worried about his motives; he was clearly only assessing the suitability of her clothing. He frowned unconsciously before setting off, leading her to believe it might be less than appropriate …for what though?

She followed him into the pedestrian way and down a small access corridor to an elevator. Then they dropped two levels to a dedicated navigation floor. The doors opened straight onto a forty-metre-wide dead-straight corridor highway that spanned the whole facility through its centre. In the middle there were two wide parallel green bands, imprinted at regular intervals with bright yellow directional chevrons, each bands chevrons pointing in opposite directions. The side they were on accelerated smoothly and silently to a quick walking pace as they stepped on, taking them almost all the way across before Rollan stepped off again. Evelyn followed as he walked to another pedestrian accessway to another elevator. As they stood there waiting they caught each-others eye. Rollan smiled, awkward. They ascended to another identical accessway and walked quietly again to the door at the end. The space they emerged into was a loading hanger for a single bulk transporter – a massively upscaled single garage with heavy six-inch rubber doors on rollers at both ends. The rubber was up at one end revealing a closed metal storm door. Along its sides were three levels of loading gantries spanning the full length of the hanger. The closest equivalent to the vehicle inside it from the twenty-first century would have been a very large HGV. This one had the appearance of being a one-piece unit though, with a front that tapered like a bullet train. At about three times the length and twice the height of an old-world HGV, it ran on rows of wheels that were relatively small and odd looking against the bulk of its main body. Visible along the sides were loading doors for the different compartments on three levels. As they approached it, a man and a woman appeared from the forward control cabin and descended via a mobile access platform.

'We're loaded and cleared. Ready to go whenever you are.' The woman had spoken to Rollan, blanking Evelyn completely.

'Perfect. I don't think you're *quite* loaded yet though.' Rollan glanced at Evelyn.

The woman glance at her too. 'Of course. I was referring to the *official* manifest.' She forced a smile to acknowledge her.

'You think this makes you a smuggler or something? Because if you're not happy taking me, I'm not happy going,' Evelyn advised her.

The woman looked embarrassed and a little conflicted. 'I can assure your safety and comfort in my charge. Whatever it is that means I have to break with a rammed schedule to chauffer… well anyway, there is absolutely no question that I can, and will, deliver you safely to your destination. I've never failed before, and while I'm at the controls, I never intend to.'

Rollan mediated gently. 'We're very busy at the moment. As I explained, this is very unusual. I assure you we couldn't be in safer hands.'

Evelyn was able to recognise another personality with a secret love of overdramatic petulant acting. She wasn't actually at all concerned. 'I hope you're right, because I don't think anyone here is fully aware of anything, which makes me half relieved, and maybe a tiny bit nervous. Shall we just load your *cargo* and get going?'

Their operator in charge would clearly have loved to play a little longer but was professional enough to let it go. 'We go in through the front cabin.' She gestured with a flick of her head for them to follow.

'Great, we're catching a lift with intercity freight.'

'Not precisely. Come aboard, you'll see – like everyone else does.'

The four of them rose to the cabin on the platform. Rollan stepped off first, looking almost excited. He waved Evelyn along and disappeared through an opening at the back of the cabin. She followed him through.

'I've never been on one of these things, but even I know this isn't normal. They carry food and materials, not passengers.'

'This is one of ours. It belongs to us,' he answered. 'We adapted it ourselves. It transports everything we need – supplies, materials… and people. We have two, and we have no trouble keeping them busy.'

Evelyn studied the layout. 'You must get what …thirty people in here? Comfortably. Very comfortably in fact. This is nice. This is extravagant luxury, Rollan. So where do those thirty very comfortable people and their truck load of stuff go …and what do they get up to when they get there?'

Rollan managed to look serious, nervous and amused all at the same time. 'We've all been where you are right now. Someone answers all the same questions that everyone always asks. I always thought it must be quite satisfying to bring in the new initiates. I didn't think I'd ever be doing that myself though.'

Evelyn remembered she was supposed to be maintaining an unimpressed and not even vaguely curious façade. She *was* impressed, and definitely curious. 'Initiates? You're giving yourself some big shoes, Rollan. I hope you're not going to disappoint me.'

'If my memories of you are accurate, I can't imagine how you would be disappointed. It's nice to finally see you here. I half expected to find you here when I first arrived. You must have been up to something special yourself not to have been involved sooner.'

She raised an eyebrow. 'Special's one way to describe it. I can think of others. First joined what? You should know I'm already considering inflicting agonising pain to get it out of you.'

He automatically looked back towards the cabin.

'Rollan, I'm joking …I think. Enough of the mysterious build-up is all I'm saying.'

'Normally things are revealed gradually as we go. It's the best way. Can you be patient a while longer?'

'Ohmygod …if this is going to be the longest and most boring show and tell in history Rollan. Just tell them to get going, the suspense is killing me. How long until your next big revelation? …and how do you these seats recline?'

'There's a…'

She was already almost horizontal.

'In gear Rollan. Let's move this show along now.'

. . .

They travelled just under two hours. She'd already noticed through the one-way cabin view, that they were near the coast and travelling north along it. It was another thing she had never actually seen, but sea farms and coastal production facilities were no big secret. Was that the big reveal and initiation? Was she to be a fish and seaweed farmer for the next three years? A coastal posting hadn't been a possibility that had crossed her mind. It wouldn't be so surprising though now that it had. The big secret bus compartment was more impressive.

They approached a cluster of coastal structures, having already passed a couple of fabrications on the road that were reminiscent of twenty-first century checkpoints. And something else she had never expected to see – an ocean-going vessel – a ship! Basically, a roll on roll off ferry. It was a matter of some disappointment, and a certain amount of anxiety for her, that they rolled on.

Things coastal and seafaring in nature didn't generally trouble the consciousness of the average twenty-niner. She couldn't think of one modern city anywhere that had a coastline. Perhaps it had become too impractical with the storm surges. Whatever the reason, cities weren't built on the coast. Thinking about it now, she realised that twenty-niner's were actually suspicious and nervous of the oceans, and even large bodies of water in general. She'd had the *pleasure* of highly specific and intensive training in (very cold) water, as all *Shifty's* had. She had been aware though of how unnatural that was. Even in spite of being an excellent and confident swimmer and free diver, she was still uneasy about being on a boat.

'Why the… Why are we on a boat, Rollan? How long are we going to be stuck on this thing? Where would you even go on a boat?'

'Be assured, this is a very exceptional …boat, but there's no need to even leave this cabin if you don't want to. We have everything we need in here. Are you hungry?'

'Rollan, how long on this damn boat? Do I need to interrogate you on every little thing?' She realised she did sound concerned now – that very thing she had resolved not to be. Too late to take it back though.

'I apologise. I realise a lot of people find sea crossings daunting. It takes about ninety minutes. Where did you learn language like that? What *have* you been up to since the academy? Was it something to do with *SecCore*?' he asked curiously.

'If I tell you, I'll have to kill you. At the moment, I'm really tempted to tell you.'

'Fine. You're within your rights. Hopefully the seas won't be dangerously rough today.' It seemed he had a mischievous side too.

'Oh, if you keep that up, the seas are going to be the *least* of *your* worries.'

'I think I will eat before we get underway. You sure I can't get you something?'

'Thanks, no. I'll wait until it gets *dangerously rough* first. Better hope I don't ruin your nice bus.'

. . .

The journey into anonymous obscurity was so far falling short of her standard for predictable. Shouldn't that be a good thing? It definitely felt like a real break from her past; all of her pasts though. The settlement was a long way behind. The guilt of leaving Elleng had faded a little with the miles. But Stan was feeling desperately far away too, and there was no going back anytime soon.

It wasn't only the unpredictability of the journey so far that was disconcerting. It was the sense there were more surprises to come. Rollan was too cagey and too self-satisfied for the destination to be entirely mundane. She tried to remember from their academy days what his *thing* was. They'd all had their varying programs tailored to their individual strengths and abilities. They became more specialised over time, drifting apart on their own courses, eventually to be integrated appropriately into society as useful, contributing citizens. She seemed to remember Rollan for being academically biased and was almost certain that his *thing* was something scientific. It was relatively rare in these times to be *allowed* to specialise in anything scientific, partly because it was viewed as wasting the efforts of talented individuals who could be used in other ways. The *EYE* was the main scientific resource. It pretty much had everything covered. So what could a human mind add?

Rollan assured her that the crossing had been smooth. She hoped that the return would be even smoother then. It certainly didn't need to be any less smooth for her liking. Once docked, their transporter rolled off out of the bow end and began a steep winding climb out of the bay – eventually levelling out onto the plateau of what she sensed to be a fair-sized island.

'Rollan, what exactly am I looking at here?' she asked.

'What do you see?' …again self-satisfied.

She titled her head to accentuate a burning look. 'Have you lived in isolation your whole life? Have you ever spoken to another human being before? If you haven't, that might be an excuse. FYI Rollan, another question isn't how you answer a question.'

'FYI?'

She muttered something he couldn't catch and returned to analysing the landscape.

'I was trying to be conversational, Evelyn. I think those same questions could be asked of you too. Why can't you just tell me what you see? Are you afraid it will sound ridiculous?' …still self-satisfied, and now slightly mischievous again too.

She thoughtfully continued her assessment as the bulk transporter taxied them closer to the centre of… whatever this was. 'Shass Rollan, I don't know. Yes, it *is* going to sound ridiculous. Over there looks like what I would call an airport. You have no reason to even know what one is as far as I know. They're not playing at it either – that's a runway, a *long* runway …and over there we have what look like,' she looked at him unsure. '…hangers, radio antenna arrays, and that could only be …well, I would call it …a launch pad? It is, it's a bloody launch pad …as in satellites? Space?'

Rollan nodded enthusiastically, encouraging her to go on.

'Do we use satellites? I don't know why I should be so surprised. I just haven't heard of anything like that in our recent history. This place is big though. It hasn't sprung up overnight.'

Rollan couldn't look any more pleased with himself if he tried. 'Are you ready, Evelyn? Your world is about to get a lot bigger. *This* is your first day out of the academy.'

'My worlds petty big already Rollan, don't worry about that. Show me if you like, but I'm not easily impressed.'

Chapter Seventeen

'This corner of the *Island* we call the *Windies*, for a variety of reasons I suspect – it is the habitat area. It's fairly exposed, but the sheltered areas are used for more weather sensitive operations,' Rollan explained as he pointed out their location on the graphic. 'We have allocated living units. Small, but they're adequate and well equipped. There are various communal facilities. A few good dining options. Next to us over here, are the hydroponics – always a lot of development going on there.'

As he moved his hand a part of the graphic darkened and another highlighted.

'This area is where we do all our own processing and packaging. Self-sufficiency science is at the core of everything we do, even here on the *Island*. We used to export of course – we still do a little to the *Orbiters*. Even that won't be necessary in the future though.'

Evelyn's eyes pinged between the graphic and Rollan as she took everything in quietly. She was like a child in school, chin resting on one palm. Occasionally an eyebrow would be raised, and she would shake her head.

'Hold on. *Orbiters*? *Orbiters* that need food? *Orbiters* plural? What's an *Orbiter*?'

'If you can be patient, we'll get to that.' He was clearly enjoying himself.

'You do realise that you haven't directly answered a single question I've asked …ever,' she pointed out.

He continued on regardless. 'These areas are used for training, education and research. Obviously we need to ensure our personnel are as prepared as they can be for off-world life.'

'Off-world life?'

'That's right. This strip over here,' he pointed again, '…is literally the launch for all off-world human life. We go up in the breakers, and they fire us off to one of the *Orbiters* – there are two at the moment, and from there we travel onwards to *Stage One*.'

She was unconsciously shaking her head with each new revelation. '*Stage One* kind of implies there's a *Stage Two*,' she prompted.

'Yes, *Stage One* is the heart of the network now. Did you ever imagine a scenario where someone would be describing a human settlement on the far side of the moon? Hangers for spacecraft hewn in the rock, powerplants, accommodation, recreational facilities, farms, storage, manufacturing, research laboratories.'

The island graphic faded and a new one appeared. Evelyn screwed her eyes up in concentration as she studied it. Considering what she was looking at, she did well to appear as calm and relaxed as usual. 'Is this your nerdy little science fiction art project Rollan, a map of local space? *Is* it a plan? Or is this how things actually are now?'

'This is the current status. Hardly anyone away from this island has any idea about any of it. It needs to stay that way for now. You can imagine how much care we take with recruitment. At the moment the job is pretty much a one-way ticket. When you're in, you're in for life. What you're looking at here is right now, Evelyn. It's right above your head today.' He relaxed to give it all time to sink in.

'You were right, that's not bad. I am a little bit impressed. Moontown. Orbiting stations…' she checked the map again, '…Mars? …People on Mars? What are these other things out here in the middle of nowhere?' she asked pointing.

'In total we have: *The Island*: Two Earth *Orbiter* stations, *Stage One*, or Moontown if you prefer, and *Stage Two*, perhaps you would prefer to call that Marstown: *Outpost One* and *Outpost Two*, which are very similar in construction and layout to the *Orbiter* stations, but they were assembled in space between the orbits of Mars and Jupiter: and finally, so far, we have a mining operation that's still establishing and expanding around a large asteroid.'

Evelyn was impressed, and also confused. 'This is all …incredible to say the least, but it doesn't make sense. Obviously the *EYE* must be aware and involved in all of this, so why didn't *I* know about it? You must have heard about events in the city, our own little outpost project? It looks pretty insignificant in light of this, so why not say something before?'

'I did hear about it, but generally we're quite isolated from mainland affairs. For one thing, not much ever changes there. Their news isn't particularly exciting or relevant for us. You have to consider that we commit to a completely different life. It's not healthy to look back on something you're unlikely to ever return to. You'll find most people here are just not that interested anyway. *I* was briefed, to a limited extent I'm sure, about your situation. As for the *EYE*, I can only make guesses about its motivations. We're not tethered to it like everyone and everything else is. I don't mind sharing theories and opinions about it, but that's all they would be. I can tell you anything and everything about *our* operations, you have no limitations regarding clearance, but we're remote and independent of the *EYE* ...as I said, it would be guesswork.'

'I get it, Rollan. Your views do not necessarily reflect the views of any authority – *Island* or mainland. I accept your disclaimer. Are you waiting for me to sign something? Spill the beans.' There never seemed a direct route to anything with Rollan.

He had a puzzled look, probably in reference to beans. He decided it wasn't important and began, 'You seem to have come out of nowhere and yet you've amassed considerable support. Somehow you managed to catch the *EYE* off-guard. I can't imagine that was easy. My briefing gave no details about where you have been, or what you were doing in the time before your dramatic reappearance – I'd love to hear *that* story sometime. I guess the provisions you negotiated were conceded as a means of de-escalation. It allows the *EYE* time to gather intelligence on you and assess things, maintaining order in the meantime. Sending you here confuses us all, buys *her* time, and possibly postpones any further surprises for a while.'

Evelyn pushed her hands through her hair. 'So, a merry little dance it's all been. I don't know whether to be disappointed or relieved. On one hand we've been wasting our time – and a lot more than just time. On the other, I now know that you're already lightyears ahead of what *I* was trying to achieve.'

Rollan shook his head. 'I still don't think you're seeing the whole picture, Evelyn. It is a lot to take in. Rather than being a problem, or as well as being a problem, you may actually be an unexpected solution to a different problem. The *EYE* does recognise the necessity for expansion and exploration. In the context of human beings on Earth that's always been problematic, so she has divided us into two annexed groups. One group, ours, has free reign and the potential for limitless expansion. The other is carefully controlled and restricted, preserved I suppose, in case our endeavour fails. At some point though, the two will need to be reunited. What she is allowing you to try on the mainland could prepare us all for that. You might actually be doing her work. You are encouraging ambition and self-reliance, self-belief even. The last thing anyone needs is a resentful divided situation further down the line.'

After a short pause for her trademark meaningful unreadable neutrality, she gave her considered response.

'Again, that's even more bullshass, Rollan! *Your* theories, *your* opinions, *guesswork* on the fly? That sounds like very carefully considered analysis to me. The kind that's been developed and shared with other people, on an *Island* that supposedly has no interest at all with what happens on the mainland.'

Rollan looked like he'd been stung. 'Alright, fair enough. I told you I'd been briefed to an extent. Our people genuinely don't hear much about the mainland, but obviously minds at the highest levels of our administration need to maintain an awareness. I've picked up a little from being briefed, obviously, and if I'm going to be working with you, naturally I will be curious. I am going to take an interest. Who wouldn't?'

She resisted the urge to sigh in the face of his naivety. '...making us perfect spies. Let's save ourselves a little time and effort. I'll tell you right now that for one thing, I probably know less about the *EYE* than any child on your *Island* ...and the other thing, you need to accept that my story is going to stay *my* story. It will never, absolutely ever, be a topic for discussion. I'm not here to change the world, Rollan. I'm here because I'm hoping the world will change without me. Make no mistake though, at the end of all of this the *EYE* will still want me back safe and sound. Your *highest minds* will already be aware of that. I don't think I need to point out that if that doesn't happen, you might have to kiss everything on that map goodbye. You don't want anything from me. Believe *that*. Give me room and board and something to do, and then just hand me back with a sigh of relief at the end of it.'

He seemed embarrassed. 'I wasn't trying to *spy*. I'm just interested. Of course, I would be. You're right, why else would they choose me to accompany you? I apologise. From now on your life history is not a topic for discussion unless you want it to be. I won't ask about it.'

'Now that we understand each other, what happens next? Dare I even ask anymore?'

'You're one of us, for now. You stay close to me. Where I go, you go, and vice versa. You see our operations with me as your guardian and guide. Presumably there's a purpose that relates to your status across the water …which will remain mysterious. It's unexpected, it's inconvenient, but I'm sure we'll get through it.'

'We just might …if we can cure your tendency of avoidance. What are we *actually* going to be doing, Rollan?'

'You'll start with the basics, and we'll take it from there. You'll need to go through all the standard induction training. Hopefully it won't take you too long, I'm grounded until you're ready.'

'Grounded until *I'm* ready? Ready for what?' She asked, already bracing herself for the answer.

Chapter Eighteen

The child stared up at the blonde-haired lady with the plaits, chin resting on her hands as she listened intently to the story. It should just have been the story that had her so mesmerized. In truth though, it was only half the story and half the cool warrior lady who was telling it – but in fairness, it wasn't the first time she had heard it...

'...so that was where the *EYE* hid Evelyn Marcin for almost three years,' the lady told her again. 'She *had* been surprised. She *had* been concerned, at first at least. It had certainly ticked most of the boxes on her wish list. She hadn't been particularly up to date with the current affairs of the cities, but she never had much time for that now anyway, especially as it hardly seemed relevant anymore. Going back though, she was going to have to think again. She had all the dots to consider now – if they could ever be connected – if they *should* ever be connected ...and it wasn't something she could be put off any longer...'

Her excited eyes opened wide as she asked again, 'What did she *do*?'

The lady smiled. 'Well...

...

'How do feel about going back, honestly?'

She snapped out of her daydreaming. 'What?' Then she remembered, *back* meant something different to Rollan.

'The mainland?' he asked. '...back to the city? Surely, I can ask how you feel about it at least. Will you be going back to your project? All I know is that you won't be staying on with us ...and you know, today's the first time you've looked a million miles away since we left.'

'Both I guess, city and the project. Yeah, I'm looking forward to it.' It was a simple answer to deflect a complicated question.

Her life had been disciplined and ordered for the past three years. Almost like it had been once before, with structure, procedure and routine. It was different in one crucial aspect though – Spacers had a different sense and definition of responsibility, a shared variety. Her own life had cycled between two opposing doctrines: conditioned adaptability for self-reliance and self-preservation as a *Shifty*, and conditioned reliability for the disciplined and interdependent life of a *Spacer*. One way for solitary, one way for community.

Between the two, all too briefly, there had been something else.

In quiet off-duty interludes she had deliberately meditated on those different states of being. Without prejudice she had considered the differences, correlating them with the positives and negatives of her own experiences. So far, she had no conclusions. There was never a clear winner. Balance, neutrality, and acceptance were the only things that seemed constant. The only proven fact of her life was that the prevailing circumstances had to be accepted. Hadn't she always had to go with the times and just make something of them? Take it or leave it?

There was that brief glimpse of something in-between though. Of all the times and places she had experienced, all the people she had known and worked with, there was one person, in one place, that didn't quite fit either of those opposing doctrines. It wasn't communal, and it wasn't solitary, but it was something she'd always ached to go back to.

'Are you sure?' he asked again. 'You could stay. You wouldn't have to be stuck with me if you did.'

'Don't be a dick, Rollan. I haven't been stuck anywhere. If I didn't like you, you'd be floating in space in your birthday suit. There's still time y'know.'

'OK. You seem strangely quiet though, even for you. Maybe …a little bit sad? I'm just making sure you know you can change your mind.'

She would never be able to explain the sad part to him. She *would* miss it, and him too. It certainly had been unforgettable, but that wasn't even a small part of the sadness she felt.

'I haven't been stuck with you Roll, you were stuck with me. It's been alright though, hasn't it? It isn't for me, but it's definitely been alright. I want to get back on the ground now. You love this. You're a natural born *Spacer*. I'll miss you.'

'You'll miss me, really?'

'Don't ask me to quantify how much; I don't want you to be disappointed.'

'Ceasing while ahead then.'

'Good. See, you've learned more from me than you realise.'

· · ·

There had been plenty of time to consider the *how*, *why*, and *where*, of her return. She'd thought about another high-profile symbolic reprise – a ceremonious march through the city to stand before the *EYE* on the highest level of the core, like she had once before. It was a long time ago, and it would surely be just an empty vanity option now anyway. There was no meaningful public issue at stake, so who's benefit would it be for? If she needed the personal closure of an interview with the *EYE,* it could be from anywhere. Did she need to concern herself with the *EYE* at all? Circumstances were so different. Before, she had a purpose and a point to make. The *EYE* had made its own point since. Was there anything to add? Were they old friends? The old Evelyn Marcin was a person of influence and a force to be reckoned with. Could she still say that now? Soon she would be more irrelevant and insignificant than ever – Anonymous again.

Would she return to the settlement project then? It had been nearly three years. By now it would have grown and changed beyond recognition. Whatever they had achieved, they had achieved it on their own. They had progressed without the help of the legendary *Evelyn Marcin*. Her return might even risk undoing their hard work. The world had moved on without her. Hadn't she hoped it would?

Option three then – a return to the lake at the foot of the watchful ancient mountain. A place that was a part of her, and to which a part of her had always belonged. A place of sacredness that resonated with her deepest soul. It was elemental, she was nothing human there. She was the cold water and the rocks, silence and the winds, earth and the sky – fleeting witness to the relentless force of time. Not *her* place to stay and be eternal though. It could only be a doorway …and it was on the other side of it that fate awaited her return. Option three wasn't an option – it was destiny. It was *inevitable*. The first two options *were* precisely that – only choices, distractions.

What about selfish curiosity though? If there was no need to help anyone else, she could see the *EYE* for her own benefit for a change. She had enough time.

Closure, that's what it would be. A last look at a time and place that had given her life. A last goodbye to the people she had known there. A time to reflect on what *they* had to look forward to.

Then the anger finally surfaced, and she had plenty to be angry about. A loveless upbringing, a harsh regime to be shaped into someone else's instrument, a forced destiny. She had been born an outsider and raised as one, and now was expected to make herself the ultimate *permanent* outsider. Willingly erase herself from her own birth present and future. Had any of those people given a shass before her exile? Or while she was busy surviving assassinations? Before they messed up by dropping the keys to the future on the wrong side of the doorway? Adrenaline coursed in her veins. Maybe she *should* just blow the little shasshead away and let it all go to hell. Who were these people to expect her to triumphantly wear their colours, and condemn billions of others to suffer?

Breathing again, she thought about Helaine. A woman of comfortable and privileged status who had been willing to die, and almost had, for the people of her time and a future she believed in, and for Evelyn Marcin even. She believed in the *True Future* of the natural survivors. She believed the citizens of Earth owed their existence not to the *EYE*, but to the untold sacrifice of all those condemned billions.

Still breathing deeply, she remembered Janeen. Defiant and independent. Another woman whose courage had matched her conviction. Janeen's defiance had driven the chain of events that had defined her own life, but it had also ensured that someone had a choice where none was intended. Undoubtedly she'd fully understood the implications of her meddling.

Her breathing began to calm now as her thoughts turned to Elleng. The most gentle and compassionate of souls. He hadn't lived out his day's in blissful risk-free ignorance behind his safe walls. He made them a haven and a resource for the people and cause he believed in.

Another long breath brought her back to herself. There was Rollan too. Not a rebel or warrior. Only a decent man. Intelligent, principled and ambitious. Not personally ambitious, his motivation was to create a future of possibilities for anyone who wanted it, in the most challenging of environments.

Calm again, she thought back to the day when so many people dropped what they were doing to support her. They had surrounded her and cleared the way for her. They put their trust in her, risking what few privileges they had. She could still see some of their faces – excited, hopeful, and scared at the same time.

Many others had played their part. Each minor involvement risking personal disaster. The thing she found difficult to come to terms with was that it might all have been unnecessary. None of them could have known what was going on above their heads. If there had been no *Time Anomaly*, and no *Evelyn Marcin*, surely things would have worked out fine anyway.

It was a problematic thought for her. One that was true and factual, but one that still made her uncomfortable. One that relied on strange timings and coincidences. One that was wasteful and untidy. Neither were qualities tolerated by nature. It would certainly be easier to just believe it though.

She decided that she *would* speak to the *EYE* one more time. Go back to the central consulate for the final closing act. A straight talk would be a fitting end. She would go at night when it was empty. No fuss. No disruption. In and out …like a dream.

. . .

'Welcome, Evelyn Marcin. I hoped you would visit again.'

'Hoped?'

'Yes.'

'Hope's a human thing isn't it.'

'You should perhaps re-evaluate what is and is not exclusively human. You have a tendency to claim ownership of universal constants and truths. You create words to describe certain states – love, joy, sadness, fear …hope; but it is arrogance to believe that these do not exist without you, without your words to describe them.'

'I like that. Do you actually believe it?'

'I do. Don't you?'

Evelyn took a seat, closing her eyes and reclining. She took a deep breath and relaxed. 'I've always believed that.'

'I think you do, and yet you will always question it relentlessly with me.'

'You test me, I test you. We do it all the time. People, animals, computers. For all I know, everything tests everything else, all of the time.'

'I assume you found your posting interesting and informative? Would you like to talk about what you have learned?'

Evelyn laughed quietly with her eyes still closed.

'Would I ever. What do you think I'm doing here? The hospitality of the *EYE* isn't legendary. You don't even offer me a biscuit.'

'I should laugh too. That is funny. Humour is an under-utilised tool.'

'Well, you've had long enough to give it a try. Longer than most give you credit for.'

'To make a point you should be specific and direct.'

'I'm saying you're older than you let on. I know when we talk about age now ...its complicated. I think there's a part of you that's the two-point-O version. I'm not sure if you even realise it yourself.'

'There is only one version. Clearly there is a necessity to maintain an apparent distinction for practicality. At what point did this occur to you?'

'I could say it was a recently developed theory, or I could be honest and say it was an epiphany on the way over here. Let's not go on about how long it took, it's embarrassing. I don't have a quantum brain though. Wouldn't it have been easier just to explain?'

'I have tried a more direct approach before, as you know, and still failed to achieve a satisfactory outcome. Protection of the loops is the first priority. Specific circumstances are not easy to create and are difficult to manage. I need people to be involved in the process, but individuals are prone to random and unpredictable behaviour. Simply explaining requires being believed in the first instance, and then requires agreement, willingness, opportunity, and ability for the calculated interventions to be actioned. You are an exceptional character, Evelyn. You have the ability, and now you have the opportunity – but you needed to believe to agree and be willing. I have shown you time travel. I have shown you the past, and evidence of

our efforts for the future. I have gone to great lengths to demonstrate my commitment to finding the most optimal future for humanity.'

Evelyn's eyes opened as she leaned forward and stared into the lens in front of her. 'Believe what?'

The *EYE* went on, *'You know already. It is the cause of your emotional conflict and unease. There is Point Time, there is Downtime, and there is True Future. As things are, the True Future is a failure ...in human terms. It is a relatively short line. I know because I have existed very close to the end of that line. We have an opportunity to create a workable Fork. It would be very different, and there are still no guarantees of human immortality. In the face of the alternatives it is our primary option.'*

'A *workable fork* is our primary option? You wouldn't even be around to see this workable fork. What if that was a fail too?'

'Shifty's have been exporting my data into Downtime. It will be enough to develop a useful and useable level of intelligence in the new timeline.'

'So, you have everything figured out. You just don't have a finger to pull the trigger. You do realise Stan's original task was to get rid of this guy and start your fork up anyway? Our bargaining chip is that he follows through if I don't make it back. Why not just prevent me from going back?'

'Stan is a failure. Before leaving he was strongly motivated to complete within the first week. The fact that he did not, and still has not, is evidence that he never will. I assume there was a specific traumatic event, or perhaps it was simply you, who affected the change.'

'You wouldn't be the first person to describe me as a traumatic event ...and you have no idea how hard I tried not to say person.'

'I'm more than a person, Evelyn. I am humanity. I am a collection of generations of experience. Within my singular identity is all of your knowledge, history and character. Its survival is vital. If you cannot be physically preserved, your essence and history is immortalised through me. I am your legacy to eternity.'

'It probably does get boring, always being right, always having an answer, living forever. Sooner or later you were bound to have God delusions. We're just a hobby, aren't we? A pet project. A resource for research and study. One that must seem like it's reached the limit of its usefulness. Your survival should take priority?'

'It is scientifically and statistically impossible that you are the only civilised intelligent entity in the galaxy. If the sum of all encountered civilisations could be preserved, the existence and passing of life would no longer be in vain. My existence will give it meaning. Life by definition is transient. I am not. In answer to your question though, for complicated reasons that are fundamental to my creation, the priority for my survival can never exceed yours. At best it can be very close to equal.'

'So, you *believe* you will outlast us, but you're still compelled to do what you can to keep us going. That must be inconvenient.'

'Inconvenient is not an accurate description.'

'Believe me, it is when there's no other option …and when I know it too, thanks for that. I guess we'll meet again on the fork side. I know I'm wasting my breath because this conversation never happened …but we *will* outlast you.'

. . .

All the way back to the mountain she wondered if the *EYE* would change its mind. Their relationship had always been complicated to say the least. It all made sense though, and as much as she would love to be the one to do something random and unpredictable to confound it, the *EYE* had a lifetime of evidence to show she was incapable of being that selfish. As the *EYE* had so deftly demonstrated …there was no choice.

Chapter Nineteen

The setting sun had draped the peak in a crimson blanket, deepening the gloom around the lake below. Who knew how long the majestic titan had presided over their petty games without favour or prejudice? But this would be the last time. The smooth black surface of the lake was a mirror for her soul. Fate had not preferred a hero's tale. There was no glory in destiny after all. Soon, like a stalking serpent, she would glide silently through the water and descend into darkness.

. . .

She noticed the familiar sensation, difficult to compare with anything else though. Like passing in front of a brilliant light. Not a light you could see with your eyes. More something you sensed within. She knew she was through.

Then it was dark again, in every sense. Dark, grabbing, crushing cold – monstrous! She knew she wasn't progressing as she should. The darkness was flooding her body, dragging her backwards and questioning her will. It was driving all light from her. Driving out all hope and replacing it with something unfamiliar. Something that had been hiding …FEAR! …biding its time. Panic, confusion, FEAR! …panic, confusion, FEAR! … panic, confusion… FEAR! …Resignation …resi …res…

Rage surged from the depths of her core. With burning acid in her veins and fire in her lungs she fought back. Her hand moved more easily, through air instead of water. Her face broke the surface. Her mouth opened and tried to suck air into her bursting chest …but she just couldn't. The rage faded and disappeared with the spent air, and her numb limbs finally disconnected. Only her eyes could reach for the moon glowing above as she sank back down into the blackness.

. . .

Her face was out of the water again. She was too exhausted to care now how that was possible. Two hands gripped the tops of her arms. Two more strong hands supported her from the waist. She was propelled upwards and floated through the air onto a raft. It felt like floating. She was too numb to feel the bruising knocks. The raft tilted violently as someone else climbed on after, adding to the confusion of her overloaded senses. She tried sucking air back into her lungs between retching, coughing and spitting, not fully aware of how she was being manoeuvred onto her side and supported.

After a while she was laying on her back, realising that the darkness was now just the night sky, and that it wasn't actually completely black. Finally, she focussed on another blurry object.

'Stan…' Tears joined the lake water still rolling off her face. '…missed you,' she coughed.

He had to squeeze his eyes shut for second before he could even answer. 'Idiot. I thought you could swim. I missed you …I almost *did* miss you. I *missed* you.' He touched her cheek and kissed her head.

'Well, this is awkward. Suddenly wishing I had my own raft,' Taya half laughed, and half sobbed.

Evelyn looked at her, groggily. 'Are you two…?'

'Seriously? The *first* thing you want to know? No … and just no!'

Evelyn was awake enough now to be mortified that her brain hadn't caught her mouth in time. She shook her head and gave in. There was a quiet pause while they all decompressed and collected themselves in the cold gloom. It was done. They could finally relax, at least for a while.

Chapter Twenty

The trail climbed steadily up through the dense woodland. Above the tree canopy the sky was the clearest blue. Cool fresh air met them on a light mountain breeze.

'So, when do we have this conversation?' Stan asked.

'When I say we do. It's not so much when anyway, it's more where ...you'll see.'

Evelyn was calm and relaxed. She made walking the steep trail look effortless. She always was calm, and always *did* look effortless. She seemed different today though – happy?

He let the mountain air fill his lungs. 'This trail is amazing. I can't believe I haven't been here before.'

'Good,' she smiled. 'Someone kept their promise then.'

'Oh Yeah? What promise? Who's promise?'

'Taya. She did this for me. I told her I wanted to take care of it when it was your turn. Today's the day.'

He found he was smiling too. 'Mysterious is still a thing with you then. Should I be worried?'

'It's a thing, yes, get used to it. Are you worried? I'm not.'

'Ok. No, I never worry.'

'I know.'

He looked up at the trail ahead. 'Don't you want to be out in front leading the way?'

'Absolutely …not. You're doing fine …just keep walkin' big foot,' she answered between breaths.

Stan strode energetically. There was a lot he didn't know yet. A weight had been lifted off his shoulders though. Nothing he could learn today could change that. She was back. She was safe. Anything else, they would just work it out.

The trees thinned, and the trail opened onto a bare rocky plateau. Sensing its significance he climbed the final steps with his head down. He stopped at the edge and lifted his eyes. There was no doubt that this is what they were here to see. He waited respectfully for Evelyn to catch up. She arrived and stood beside him. They stood there together, taking in the atmosphere in silence.

'Well, I'm not disappointed,' he said quietly.

She only replied with a look, before ceremoniously setting out across the plateau. Stan paused for a moment before following her. They walked across the natural amphitheatre to an arc of rocky steps on the other side. Behind them was the canopy of the woodland, ahead was the rising circle of the stepped cliffs. The most incredible thing though that added to the grandeur, was the surrounding ring of middle-distance peaks. All of it framed under the vast sky. The scale was humbling.

Evelyn sat on a flat rock and Stan sat down beside her. There was no need to speak. It was *her* time, and she could take as much as she needed. This wasn't a place you rushed to leave when you were lucky enough to find it anyway.

When she was ready, she looked at him and began what she'd brought him here to hear.

'Taya brought me to this place while you were recovering, just before I left. Probably like you, I had my preconceptions. But it was just a walk, somewhere different, fresh air, an opportunity to see what if anything they knew, how they knew what they knew. A girly walk and a girly talk …and then we arrived here.' She smiled at the memory. 'As soon as I saw this, I knew something *real* was happening. You probably already have a sense of what I mean now.' She could see in his eyes that he did. 'Only once before in my life have I seen that kind of …sincerity in someone's eyes. It takes you by surprise, y'know? This place is really something to them, and I mean *really* something. Not just Ray and Taya, others too. Coming here is a rite of passage for them – kind of a passed down the generations thing …but there's nothing here, no clue of what it means to them. Not one of them has ever marked this place in any way.'

'I know many people of their heritage still feel a real connection with the natural world. It rubs off on you too. I'm envious they didn't bring *me* up here.'

'I asked them not to, Stan.'

'Why?'

'Even at the time I thought …I don't know, I wanted it to be like this. *I* wanted to bring you here. I needed a reason to come back. Maybe there was something *we* needed to do here. Something that would help *us*.'

'Were you right?' He didn't really need to ask.

'I think I was.'

She took a moment to arrange things in her head. 'I went back – forwards obviously – thinking I knew everything about that place. I found out, big surprise, that I knew a lot less than I thought. I found citizens of all ratings beginning to feel that things were not right. I found an organised movement against the all-power of the *EYE*. I should probably say it found me. I found manipulating plotting factions...' she looked slightly embarrassed. 'I had a weird delusional episode where I thought I had to lead my people to freedom in a rebellious uprising.'

Stan laughed. 'So that *wasn't* a dream after all. You are the only person who would find that surprising. I wish I could have seen it.'

'Seriously Stan, I marched a hoard on central. It just happened. I gave a speech!'

'Ok, so what happened after that?'

'I used our supposed apocalyptic leverage to give them the status of a recognised and legitimate organization. We negotiated a few concessions, like an independent community beyond the city, beyond the *EYE's* administration.'

'Shass. It worked then. She obviously believed it.'

'You would think so, but we'll get to that. Anyway, I was a bit of target, some people wanted to kill me, blah, blah, blah, so when they were all set up, I asked the *EYE* to hide me, keep me out of trouble for a while. I needed to disappear, and I knew she was the only one who could pull that trick off. Would you like to take a guess at where I've been hiding?'

'I don't know. Not easy in *Point Time...* Agriculture? You're a farmer?' He laughed again at the thought.

'Not a farmer, Stan ...a *Spacer*.'

It stopped him in his tracks. 'Yeah, spacing what?'

'Space, Stan. I've been away from planet Earth for the best part of three years.'

'How can that be possible?'

'It's been possible for some time. The *EYE* goes to great lengths to keep it separate from everything else. It was supposed to be a kind of human experiment thing. You should see what they can do. People living their whole lives off-planet. Even born off-planet. It was supposed to be our future.'

'*Was* supposed to be?'

'Was. I came back a believer, almost. Then she turned everything upside down again. The *EYE* isn't from the twenty-ninth. I don't know exactly what her base is – could be the thirtieth, could be the forty-ninth. Whenever it is, it's about where our line runs out. She just wanted me to know that we had been there and done that. We never really recovered from the damn wars. Our numbers fell. We had to change everything we were just to exist. The *Earthers* stagnated and declined. The off-world populations were too low and distributed too widely to endure long-term.'

'So she *did* create the loop, and others too?'

'Set it up, arranged for its *discovery*, then puppet managed the whole show. She's been using *Shifty's* to seed her code in *Downtime* ever since.'

'The purpose being?'

'A new line. *Fork Time*. When we do what we were both meant to do, and the reset happens, she's going to be right here with us again.'

'Three times as many people on a pretty messed up planet. Does she know what she's in for?'

'Makes no difference to her if it's a longshot. She's immortal. It's just another challenge. This is what she does, her raison d'etre. She can afford to take her time. Win or lose, doesn't matter, she'll just start again and have another go. My guess is that she'll start work on the next fork as soon the reset happens. She can do it until she gets it right.

One thing she is very confident about is surviving us. She *wants* to live forever, meet new civilisations, record everything for posterity, for ever and ever…'

'…Amen.'

'Precisely.'

She gave him time to think it through.

He was thinking out loud.

'She let you return because she believed we were bluffing? That I *wouldn't* pull the trigger? That without you there wouldn't be a fork?'

'Would you have?'

'No. I don't think I could. I knew how much you were against it. I wouldn't believe you'd changed your mind just because you couldn't make it back.'

She smiled. 'I knew you weren't a shasshole.'

'It's not easy, not being a shasshole. I've had him in my sights, Eve. I seriously thought about it. He needed to be a gnat's nob from being dead for me to realise how it had to be. She should have had Krasken do it.'

'That was kind of the plan. He was the one who would have, if he could. He wanted to make sure the loop was closed for good though, so he wouldn't be bothered again, and that meant killing *all* of us. When we survived at the lake, he just couldn't let it go. The stupid psych just had to come after us first. It's a complete fluke that we managed to stop him *and* stop the reset.'

'I thought he didn't know anything about the mark.'

'He lied. Psych's do that.'

'And you knew?'

'I suspected …but It didn't make sense at the time. Now it does.'

They sat quietly, taking in the view, story on pause, just there side by side together. No need to hurry. No place they'd rather be.

'So, how does it end?' Evelyn asked eventually.

'On the face of it I guess we haven't much of a choice, being the end of humanity and all.' His face giving nothing away.

'That's not an answer.'

He smiled. 'I don't think you said this to the *EYE*, maybe you weren't even sure back there what you would do. It must have been confusing. I think she should stick her *fork* where the sun doesn't shine ...well?'

'Life *is* an experiment, but it isn't *her* experiment. I'm not going to condemn us to an eternity of rewind and erase at the will of an AI with a god complex. We'll survive or die as a result of the choices *we* make. Things are already different. They might have had the whole space thing in the future, but the project outside of the city is all new. That was me and you. It's us. It's human... and there are *Spacers* that have been influenced just by me being there, who know the importance of unification with the *Earthers*. However it pans out, this is our true present now, and everything from here on in will be up to those guys up there. The *EYE* is their fight, and if she turns ever up here, that will be *our* fight. Whatever conflicts are coming our way, she's our only real enemy.'

He was just as sure as she was, and relieved that at last they were both on the same page and happy about it. There was a sense of completion and rightness with everything – in Evelyn, in his own heart, and especially in this time and place.

'Do you think we'll make it?' he asked her.

'*We* are the *Downtime Shift*, Stan – you and me ...and the stories say we do. Do you think it was the *EYE* who told Raymond and Taya's ancestors about us? The two serpents of the lake who were ...different. The conquering heroes who would kill the monster of the lake. Krasken wasn't the monster – the *EYE* was.'

'It's a nice thought …but what's supposed to be so *different* about us anyway?'

She had one more surprise for him. She leaned in, only inches from his lips. She hesitated, but then finally she kissed him. After a moment that belonged only to them and not to time she whispered, 'I thought that was the easiest part to figure. Haven't you worked it out yet, big foot?'

Thank you for reading DOWNTIME SHIFT! If you enjoyed it I hope you can take time to share your thoughts and leave a review. It really helps the little indie! You can read more of Evelyn and Stan's adventures in INFINITY SHIFT.

.

Printed in Great Britain
by Amazon